Julia's head was spinning. She thought she could hear voices saying malicious words, chanting them over and over. A sudden gust of wind made the whole house tremble. At the same instant, as the house shuddered, there was the sound of a door closing.

The room seemed frozen and deserted. Then a movement arrested her attention—a slow movement, a dim white square shape rising slowly. . . .

The hands, the monsterous white hands! As she stared, one of them moved in a grotesque beckoning gesture.

The cold within her was rising dizzily to her head making her feel faint. Unable to shift her eyes away she took another step backward and stumbled. Then the cold entirely enveloped her and quenched the day.

# Dorothy Eden
## Bride by Candlelight

ace books

A Division of Charter Communications Inc.
A GROSSET & DUNLAP COMPANY
1120 Avenue of the Americas
New York, New York 10036

# ONE

THE snowflakes fell with almost inaudible thuds against the window pane, like gloved fingers tapping. The wind blew straight from the mountains. Beyond that whirling world of whiteness Julia could imagine the towering cruel slopes, and the fancy came to her that the mountains were like people whose hearts had frozen, long ago, and who now revelled in the howling wind and the cold of which they were the authors. The little round tussocky hills that loved the sunlight; gathering it over them in a yellow coverlet, were obscured, the thorny grey matagouri bushes had become full of an improbable dignity.

Julia thought of the little blue lakes that lay in the hollows of the hills. They would be snowed over now, all their blueness quenched. They would be shrivelled and pinched and colourless, like her own heart. Like her heart today, because she was so frightened.

Perhaps it was only because they were completely shut-in by the storm that she was so afraid. She was suffering from claustrophobia. Because she could not escape from the house she imagined it was dangerous to stay. If the sun had been shining and she had been able to walk out perhaps she would not have gone. When she could have gone a week ago she would not. Perhaps it was only the snow that was making her so frantic.

Nevertheless, she must finish the letter to Uncle Jonathan so that if anything did happen. . . . But *nothing* would happen. It was sheer imagination.

Her chilly hand moved the pen over the paper.

I want you to know, Uncle Jonathan, that although you may feel you persuaded me to come here to marry Paul, I would still have done so without your help. I wanted to come. Paul was the first man I ever loved, and I always hoped to marry the first man with whom I fell in love. Perhaps I am just a silly romantic. I can't tell. For I still don't know whether I shall ever marry Paul or not.

Harry may stop us.

Did you know that Paul had a brother Harry? He died in Australia several months ago of pneumonia. He was only twenty-six. They say he died. Yet I am sure he is in this house. I have never seen him. Then how can I be sure he is here? There are various ways, the things Georgina says, the voices I have heard, the way Nita behaved, the notes that are put under my door in the night. If there is ever another note I shall go mad. I can't bear them any more, they are so stupidly demoralising, and there is no longer anyone I can tell about them because I don't know whom I can trust. The funny thing is that I am sure it is Harry who doesn't want me to marry Paul. If the snow hadn't come and shut us in—we may not be able to get to the church tomorrow—something else would have happened. Perhaps something worse.

I am not just being stupid and imaginative. Too many odd things have happened. The worst thing of all is that now I am not sure about Davey. No one seems to know very much about him, not even Paul. Or if Paul does he doesn't tell me anything. At first I talked a lot to Davey because I was lonely and nervous, and he seemed such a sane sensible person, even if he did despise me and call me the Queen of Sheba. He wasn't exactly friendly but I did trust him.

Now, with the things that have happened, I am so afraid that Davey is——

Julia's hand stopped dead, the nib of her pen stabbing the paper rigidly.

There was something protruding beneath her door, a folded scrap of paper.

She sat staring at it. She knew it was useless to run to the door and fling it open and see who was disappearing down the passage. There would be no one there. Never once had she heard a footstep. The folded slips of paper

just appeared beneath her door as if they came there of
their own accord.

Even that first one, in the hotel, had just been lying on
the desk, the reception clerk said, as if it had materialised
out of thin air. In this letter she was writing to Uncle
Jonathan, Julia thought slowly, she ought to tell him everything from the beginning so that if it happened that
she never saw him again he would know the events that
had brought her to this state of fear and apprehension. . . .

It was the letter from Paul that had brought her to New
Zealand, that combined with Uncle Jonathan's persuasion.
Julia was very dear to him, Uncle Jonathan had said, but
he was old and sick. She had no other family, and when
he died she would be left alone. A villa on the French
Riviera and an adequate income were of some value, but
a husband, especially a fine young man like the New
Zealander, Paul Blaine, was of a great deal more importance. And this was not because he was prejudiced in
Paul's favour by reason of the fact that once he had been
deeply in love with a young English girl, Georgina Heriot,
who was now Paul's grandmother.

Uncle Jonathan had given Julia a love for French literature
and a home in the sunshine of the Mediterranean with all
its attendant pleasures. But very few young people came
to their home. Julia was lonely. She was inclined to think
too much about her meeting with Paul three years ago
in war-time England, and to fret about his silence which
could have meant either that he had forgotten her or that
he was dead.

When the letter came Uncle Jonathan said she must go.
But she had meant to go, anyway.

During the four weeks' journey out she had occasionally felt nervous and apprehensive. She had wondered if Paul
would be the way she remembered him. She had wondered, too, if the excitement of seeking her husband on the
other side of the world had been of more importance to
her than her feelings for Paul himself. But it was not until
she waited in the hotel room in Timaru, the seaside town
in the South Island of New Zealand, that was the gate-
way to the lonely tussock-ridden country stretching to the

7

foot of the Alps where Paul's sheep station was situated, that she began to feel frightened.

She kept looking at the door, waiting for it to open. A dozen times she had imagined what Paul would say, but never had she been able to think what she would answer.

The answer would come spontaneously, she told herself, just as most of her actions did. If she could come half way across the world to marry a man because he had written her one irresistible letter, she need scarcely worry about her first words to him.

In any case he would probably kiss her so that she could not speak. And everything would be completely right.

At any time now the door would open. Julia forced her eyes away from its depressing pale chocolate surface, and turned to the window to watch the road. This led through a cutting and up a hill. The cliffs on either side of the cutting were clay, as yellow as dandelions, and beyond the houses were perched on the hillside like nesting seabirds. It was early spring and the flowering trees were white ghosts and pale pink clouds. Soon after her arrival everything had been vivid and exciting, with the strong spring sunlight, the dancing blue sea, the sea-faded colours of the town. And the anticipation. The excitement of a new town, a new country, mingled with her anticipation of Paul's arrival.

For an hour, two hours, she had been in a happy dream. But now the sun had set, all the colour had gone out of the sea, it was very cold and she was tired. She was so tired that she would have cried had she not always scorned tears, and fought against them as a sly and humiliating enemy. Even alone and unseen she would not allow herself to weep.

Something had happened to prevent Paul arriving. He had sent that message to the ship in Wellington telling her to wait for him at the George Hotel in Timaru, because it was a four-hour drive to Heriot Hills, and if anything delayed him he didn't want her forced to hang around a railway station.

Consequently, she had gone to the George Hotel, and for the first two hours she hadn't minded at all. She had thought the lounge with its turkey-red carpet, its shabby

8

comfortable chair, and its air of cosy gloom, could very easily have belonged to one of the seaside hotels at Bournemouth or Littlehampton or Eastbourne where she used to be taken for holidays. It had just been transported to the antipodes, along with herself, and with it, too, had come all the ecstatic excitement and glamour of holidays in a real hotel by the sea.

For two hours she was a mixture of a child on holiday in a new intriguing place, and a nervous young bride-to-be. Her friendship with Paul in England had been for so short a time. When she tried to think back over what it had been, it was all concentrated in her mind in one lovely new sensation of tenderness, excitement, growing love. What had there been between them? A night dancing, an old song, a drive along the sea coast as dawn showed in a pale primrose line, a withered spray of lily of the valley, a half dozen letters of a shy formality that could have meant everything or nothing.

Then the three-year-long silence during which, she now knew, Paul had been in and out of hospitals and undergone a series of skin grafts for war wounds.

No wonder, when that surprising letter had come and she had impulsively announced her intention of agreeing to Paul's proposal, her friends, apart from Uncle Jonathan, had told her she was crazy.

Crazy. . . . Julia looked round the drab darkening room. Was she? She hadn't seemed so, or perhaps she had, in a purely delightful way, until now. Now it was no longer an altogether amusing craziness.

Supposing Paul didn't come. He had wanted her to marry him in Wellington. He had sent a cable to the ship asking her to do that. She had had the impression that he meant to have the parson waiting at the foot of the gangway. After his long silence the impatience had been flattering, but a little puzzling. She cabled back, refusing, saying that she wanted to be taken to Heriot Hills first, to meet his family and to become accustomed to her new home.

She hadn't any uncertainties about her feelings for Paul. Ever since getting that letter she had been in a state of dreamy delight. *My dear love. . . . You are my day*

9

*and night. . . .* Paul had said those things, shy uncommunicative Paul!

She remembered his steady blue eyes and longed to be in his arms. Yet she was not ready to marry him in Wellington. She mixed caution with her craziness. She wanted to see her home first, and after all there was her elaborate trousseau which must be displayed with all the background of a real wedding.

Perhaps subconsciously she was providing herself with a loophole for escape.

That was quite silly, of course. Yet had it not been justified? For strangely enough Paul had not met her in Wellington. There had only been the note telling her to come to Timaru and wait at the hotel.

Now she was here, and still he had not come.

It must be the storm that had held him up. The girl at the reception desk, when Julia had enquired whether she could put a telephone call through to Heriot Hills, had told her that the telegraph wires were down. There had been a bad storm in the high country the previous night, and communications were temporarily cut.

"There's some flooding," she had told Julia, "but cars are getting through. I should think your friend would arrive."

Had Paul been held up on a flooded road, or had he mistaken the day? Julia refused to panic. She had asked the girl at the desk for a room, since it now looked as if she might have to spend the night there.

One more night, after the weeks of travelling, didn't matter much, she told herself. It was the tiredness that was getting under her guard, making her suspicious, uneasy, homesick. Had Georgina Heriot felt like this when she had arrived here nearly sixty years ago? Had she thought regretfully of home, of the old dull but dearly familiar ways, perhaps even of Jonathan whom she had rejected. Had the sharp strong sunlight, the bare hills, the sweeping winds of this country seemed too alien to her? If they had she would never have admitted it. She had quarrelled with Uncle Jonathan and left him for the New Zealander, Adam Blaine. She would have been too proud to confess she had made a mistake and come back. Perhaps she hadn't made a mistake.

But Uncle Jonathan, convinced that one day she would admit she still loved him, had dedicated his life to waiting for her to return to him. Even when she and Adam Blaine had established their home, called it Heriot Hills and started their family, Uncle Jonathan had refused to believe in the permanence of her absence.

Poor Uncle Jonathan. His last words to her had been, "I'm so happy you're going. Tell Georgina I still love her."

She had known that he was feeling that in a strange and vicarious way his long faithfulness was being rewarded. His dearest niece was going to marry the grandchild of his old love. It was an unexpected but deeply satisfying fulfillment to his life.

A baby in the next room had begun to cry. Julia came away from the window and switched on the light. By electricity the room looked even more dreary and anonymous. She preferred the growing and melancholy darkness, and switched off the light again. She had begun to think of that silly letter someone off the ship had sent her in Wellington.

*Think well before you marry Paul Blaine. Are you sure he really loves you?* It was signed "A well-wisher."

Obviously it had been the work of that foolish but rather nice Johnnie Weir who had followed at her heels during the entire voyage. Only someone off the ship would know the hotel at which she had planned to spend the night. The letter had been handed in at the desk.

It had been a stupid thing to do. People who wrote anonymous letters were not funny. And of course Paul really loved her or he would not have sent for her.

What was wrong with that baby next door? It sounded as if it were forsaken. Perhaps she could go in to it. That would be two forsaken people together. Even as she made that decision a door clicked and a moment later the baby stopped crying.

Almost at once a tap at her own door made her start. Paul! She hurried to open the door.

The rather dull-faced girl from the reception desk stood there.

"A letter has just been left for you, Miss Paget," she said, and handed Julia the unstamped envelope.

Julia closed the door slowly, staring at the handwriting. It was peculiarly familiar, yet she couldn't think where she had seen it before. She tore the envelope open and suddenly her hand began to tremble. For the note was written in the same large black print as the one she had received in Wellington. The writer could not be Johnnie after all. Johnnie had stayed in Wellington. It couldn't be Johnnie's stupid joke. Perhaps it was not meant to be a joke at all.

The writing this time said bluntly,

*If you marry Paul Blaine you are deliberately running into danger. Think well.*

Rather breathlessly Julia crumpled the sheet of paper back into the envelope. She stood reflecting for a few moments, then she went downstairs.

The hotel no longer seemed the comfortable, happy, exciting, turkey-red place of her childhood. People stared at her too closely. Or did she imagine it? Wasn't it in all their faces that there was the girl whom Paul Blaine had sent for, and now didn't want?

She went to the reception desk and attracted the attention of the dull-faced clerk.

"Excuse me. Can you tell me who left this letter?"

The girl looked surprised. "I don't know. I didn't see. Doesn't it say?"

"It isn't signed," Julia said casually. "I suppose it's someone who expected me to know their handwriting."

The girl had lost interest. She had got out her compact and was powdering her nose. It was six o'clock; no doubt her finishing time.

"How queer," she said indifferently. "It was lying on the counter. I didn't hear anyone come. You don't, on the carpet. It wouldn't have been there more than a few minutes."

"Oh. Well, thank you."

Julia turned away helplessly. So someone who knew something—or was it just mischief—could not be far from here. But where? And how in Wellington yesterday, and Timaru, a town in another island, today? Was she being followed?

"Dinner's at seven," she heard the girl at the desk saying.

She didn't get ready to go down to dinner. It had been

12

going to be such a happy evening with Paul. Now, for-lorn and just a little more frightened all the time, she knew she could not face dinner alone. She decided to go to bed. Whether the arrival of a prospective bridegroom were imminent or not, she would pull the sheets over her head and sleep. Then she would wake refreshed and be again the girl Uncle Jonathan admired, impulsive, ready for any experience, frightened of nothing.

First, for reassurance, she would unpack her wedding dress and re-read Paul's letters.

*If you marry Paul Blaine you are deliberately running into danger.* How utterly stupid. What was nice, shy, gentle Paul going to do to her? Make her unbearably unhappy? Murder her?

New Zealanders, she thought, must like playing cruel senseless jokes. Or one of them must.

She lifted the wedding dress out of the suitcase and shook out its folds. And then it was like the blossoming trees she had seen on the hillside, ethereal, immaculate as snow.

Julia began to smile to herself. The lovely thing. She imagined the girl who would be in it, herself and yet not herself, the pure, not quite of this world creature who would startle herself as much as Paul.

Suddenly she wished she was getting married in her grey suit and her favourite red tam o'shanter with the long tassel. That would be more honest.

But no. She had to wear this dress for the look it would bring to Paul's eyes. One had to introduce these moments of utter perfection into marriage. Forever afterwards Paul would remember his first sight of her in the white dress, and she would remember the look in his eyes.

There! The magic of the dress was working. She had almost forgotten her state of anxiety and depression. When she was in bed she would begin Paul's letters.

*My dear love. . . . This silence has not been my wish. . . . I had longed to write to you sooner. . . .*

In bed Julia fell asleep with the letter slipping out of her relaxed fingers. She dreamt that Uncle Jonathan was rapping on the bedposts with his sharp yellow knuckles, saying, *"You must go! You must go!"* while she herself was crying, *"Am I crazy? Who is Paul Blaine?"*

"Much less crazy than you think," said Uncle Jonathan, knocking emphatically.

The sound became so loud that Julia awoke, and realised that the knocking was no dream but a reality. It was at the door of her room.

Paul at last! She leapt out of bed and ran to the door. She need not have wondered how she was going to greet him, for as she opened the door her spontaneous feet took her gaily into her caller's arms.

"Oh, Paul! You were so long!"

"Hold on a minute," said a strange voice. "This is extremely pleasant. But I'm not Paul."

At first she thought she would never get over the embarrassment of having flung herself, in her nightdress, into the arms of a strange man. Waking from her dream like that, she had been so sure it would be Paul. It was dark in the passage and she could not see the man clearly, as she fervently hoped he could not see her.

She backed into the room and slammed the door. Then she opened it six inches and said belatedly,

"Who are you? Haven't you come to the wrong room?"

"Are you Miss Paget?"

She still could not see his face. She had the impression that he was laughing at her. It made her curt.

"I am."

"Then I have a letter for you."

"Not another!" she gasped. "Wait a minute."

She extricated a housecoat from her half-unpacked suitcase and put it on, then switched on the light and said, "Come in. Give me the letter."

Without glancing at him she took the envelope from his outstretched hand and tore it open. The sheet of paper had Paul's signature at the bottom. She read swiftly,

Dear Julia,

I hope you have arrived safely. I am afraid we shall have to ask you to stay in Timaru for a few days. I have had a cursed accident, twisting my ankle so that I am tied like a hen to a white line, and we have had a storm that has cut off the electric light and telephone. To put it mildly, we're in a hell of a mess. Besides, I

14

wanted to get the place tidied up before you came. I had planned for this to be done while we were honeymooning in the North Island, but as you preferred to be married from here my mother insists that the house has to be dressed up.

I'm infernally sorry that I couldn't meet you because of this accident. I am sure they will make you comfortable at the George for a week or so. I'll be in the minute I'm able to get about.

I am sending this note with the shepherd, Davey Macauley. Even without the help of his name he is a learned bloke. Get him to buy you a meal.

All my love, Paul

Julia's first feeling was one of intense anger. So the very first moment of her arrival she was being tossed casually to the shepherd. It was unbelievable. How could Paul *do* that to her? It just didn't fit in with his previous ardent letters, his impetuous desire to be married the moment she stepped off the ship. Was he behaving in this cold way because he was angry with her for having crossed his wishes?

The Paul she had known could not have been vindictive. No. The answer came to her instinctively. Paul hadn't written that letter. It was too queer and cold and indifferent. It might have been a business arrangement about a consignment of sheep. It just wasn't a letter from a bridegroom to his prospective bride. *You are my day and my night.* . . .

The warmth came back into Julia's heart. She looked with confidence at the strange young man who stood in the doorway.

"You are Mr. Macauley?"

He nodded.

"Paul suggests that you buy me a meal. But I think we ought to leave at once."

"Leave?" he said. His voice had a pleasant deep intonation. He seemed to be a respectable if not particularly friendly young man.

"Yes," she said. "You are going back to Heriot Hills tonight, aren't you? If you are, I'm coming with you."

He seemed taken aback.

"Oh, I don't think you should do that, Miss Paget."

15

"Why not? Is there something there I shouldn't see?"

Did he hesitate ever so little?

"It's just that it's a long way and the roads are bad. It will take four to five hours with the flooding. If the streams have come down any more we might not get through."

"I'm prepared to risk that," she said decisively. "I'm coming with you."

## TWO

THERE was no stopping her. It was useless to tell her that Paul had written that letter, and to suggest that she compare the handwriting with that of previous letters. She only said, "Yes, it does look the same, but a clever person can imitate handwriting. Paul wouldn't write that."

She made him think of that couplet about the goddess Ate: *Her feet are tender for she sets them not on the ground, but on the heads of men.* He imagined he could feel the weight of them already. He let women do nothing to his heart, but his senses inevitably responded to feminine charm. And this girl was extremely charming, as one might have expected when Paul Blaine wanted her. Her hair was tousled and there were fatigue marks under her eyes. But there she was, with her dark fly-away hair, her shell-pink skin offset by eyes so deep a blue as to seem black, and a square jaw that was almost belligerent. Her figure, as he had felt it, momentarily and accidentally, through her night-dress, left no grounds for criticism. A shade thin for her height, perhaps. That was one surprising thing. Paul liked more voluptuous women. He also liked them fairly complaisant to his wishes.

What was he going to say if they arrived at midnight, with things the way they were? It might be amusing to see what did happen.

In any case this girl, who had trustingly come across the

world to marry Paul, was entitled to know the true state of things. Whatever the truth was. . . .

The final thing was, of course, that the owner of that small square chin was not going to be thwarted over a desire. The likeness came to him of a sea-pink, improbably fragile, yet surviving with an astonishing vitality cold winds and poverty-stricken soil. He began to smile sardonically at his unwittingly sentimental imagination, and he heard her crisp voice,

"Is there something funny, Mr. Macauley?"

He was not quite used to being called by that name yet. Somehow it sounded stranger still and rather foolishly pretentious on her lips.

"Nothing at all. But if you're coming with me we'd better start. It's a long drive. And I have some things to pick up in town. Among them, candles."

"I won't take five minutes if you'll help me pack this dress."

She took the filmy white dress from the wardrobe and spread it on the bed. Davey looked at it in amazement. It was like a frothing white wave. It would be as incongruous, at Heriot Hills, as champagne at a shepherd's supper.

"Are you planning to take that?"

"Indeed I am. It's my wedding dress."

She began expertly to compress the white billows into a transferable size. She paused to give him a look.

"What's the matter? Don't you like it? You should. It's a Lanvin."

"At Heriot Hills," he said slowly, "in that, you're going to look like a new-born lamb."

"Your mind must run on sheep, Mr. Macauley. Give me that case, will you? This dress isn't the only pretty thing I have. I hope you have plenty of room in your car. I have twelve bags and a cabin trunk. My Uncle Jonathan bought my trousseau for me. He insisted on it being a good one. I mustn't disgrace Paul."

"My goodness gracious!" Davey muttered. "The Queen of Sheba, to say the least."

"Well, I only pray Paul isn't like Solomon." She gave him

her clear dark blue glance. "But of course he isn't. That's quite comical to think of with Paul."

"Is it?" Davey muttered. But in her pre-occupation over packing the fabulous dress she didn't seem to hear his non-committal answer.


# THREE


As they went Julia said blithely, "I can tell you I shall be delighted to get out of this place. Hotels are so horribly anonymous."

That word brought back the thought of those peculiar letters, and she took a quick glance at the young man with her, wondering if he was the sort of person in whom one could confide. It came to her all at once how very alone she was, and for a moment her heart wavered again.

Could the same person have written all three letters, even the one purporting to be from Paul? She didn't think so, because the anonymous ones were printed, whereas the one from Paul was written in what certainly looked like his own handwriting. Perhaps, she began to reflect more soberly, he was in such pain from his sprained ankle that he could do no more than put on paper the barest instructions. Poor darling, how pleased he would be to see her so unexpectedly.

Yet in spite of her sane reasoning she could not convince herself that Paul had really written that letter.

Nevertheless, she refused to be depressed. Something had happened at last. In a few hours she would see Paul. She was on fire with excitement.

She scarcely noticed Davey Macauley's aloof unfriendli-ness. She had been so silent all day that now she had to talk. As the road winding into the hills slipped away be-hind them, and all the country that could be discerned was pinpointed in the car's headlights, a clump of the squat dark macrocarpa trees, a wooden cottage overgrown with geraniums and ivy, the glimmer of water that lay in pools by the roadside, a glimpse of a hill's bare slope, Julia chattered. Partly she talked because it relieved her, partly because already she was conscious of an instinctive shrinking from the loneliness of the countryside. It was the sound of the wind that made it so lonely, and the occasional glimpse of a polar white mountain crest.

"And who," she said suddenly, in the midst of an account of the voyage out from France, "do you think would write me stupid anonymous letters? You know the kind of thing. 'Beware! You are playing with fire.' "

At last she had his full attention.

"Did someone write that to you?"

"Not exactly those words, but the meaning was similar. It's awfully like cheap melodrama, isn't it? The Black Hand sort of thing."

"How long has this been happening?"

"Oh, only since yesterday. I got one letter in Wellington, and one this evening in Timaru. I thought at first it was from someone on the ship who was playing a joke. But the one tonight made me think I was being followed. Is there anyone who would be jealous of my marrying Paul?"

"A woman?"

"Who else?"

He hesitated. "I would hardly know. I have only been at Heriot Hills for three months."

"Isn't three months long enough to notice things?" she said lightly.

"I have my work to do."

"You're very non-committal, Mr. Macauley."

"Am I? By the way, most people call me Davey."

Julia supposed that after one had flung oneself, practically unclad, into a man's arms, the basis of first names was inevitable. But Davey Macauley hadn't made the suggestion with any show of friendliness. It was almost as if being addressed formally made him uncomfortable. Perhaps he thought Macauley was an unlikely name for a shepherd. If it came to that, he did not behave in the least the way she had imagined a shepherd would. He was too alert and contained. For all his aloofness and appearance of disinterest she felt that he would miss nothing. So he must know all about the household at Heriot Hills.

"Would this person in a crude sort of way be trying to frighten me off?" she persisted.

"I wouldn't know about Mr. Blaine's private affairs."

"Oh, come! Wouldn't you have noticed if some silly girl was breaking her heart over him. Although from what I remember of Paul he wouldn't be that kind of person. He was too shy. But I suppose in three years one can change."

Again she was surprised at herself for talking in this confiding way to a man whom she had only just met, and who was merely an employee at Heriot Hills. But Paul had casually entrusted her to his care. So he must be someone of some standing. Anyway, his voice and his manner showed that. And, like someone drunk with words after a long silence, she had talked too much to stop.

"My Uncle Jonathan was the only person who thought I wasn't crazy to come to New Zealand to marry a man I had known only for a few days. I suppose it was really because of him that I came. There might have been too many difficulties to overcome otherwise."

"You mean you might not have had a trousseau?"

She caught the flavour of sarcasm in his voice.

"That is something," she said blithely. "Nice clothes mean a lot to a girl. You think I've come out to have a smart wedding and show off my things?"

"It could look that way," he said indifferently.

She laughed good-humouredly.

"I suppose it could. But I do happen to be in love. That would be something, too, wouldn't it?"

"Oh, indeed."

He *couldn't* be a shepherd, not with that neat sardonic manner. She was enjoying this dry interchange of words. She would tell Paul about it, saying, "At first I was mad with you for sending your shepherd to fetch me, but then I realised you knew I would have an amusing journey."

"Uncle Jonathan has a passion for French writers," she said, "Balzac, Anatole France, Flaubert. He lives in them. You know, the French still have marriages of convenience. Uncle Jonathan thinks that is so tidy and civilised. He felt he was arranging one with Paul and me when he helped me to come. But of course he realised the difference with us was that we were in love."

"Then it must have been a long three years for you since you last saw Mr. Blaine."

How could she tell him that she had only really fallen in love with Paul since getting that last letter, that unexpected tender passionate letter that said all the things she ever wanted a man to say? He would laugh at that confession.

"Oh, it was. Terribly long. But Paul explained about that. He had been in hospital a lot of the time having skin grafts, and he didn't think it was fair to write to me until he knew that he would be all right. He had bad face wounds, did he tell you? I completely understand how he felt. He would be so sensitive about it until he was presentable again." Suddenly she was saying a little uncertainly, "I suppose I shall recognise him?"

"I didn't know him in the past," Davey said. "He has only faint scars now." He added in his slightly contemptuous voice, "You don't need to be nervous, Miss Paget."

"Apparently I don't. Especially since some woman seems to be crazy about him. Tell me honestly, Davey, have you any idea who she would be?"

"I'm afraid not."

"Oh. All right. I'll find out. The silly little scrap. Then would you tell me what the household at Heriot Hills is. I know so little about Paul's family, really. He has never talked much about it. But then we've scarcely had time. I only knew him for those few days when he was in England on leave."

"I suggest you wait until you get there, Miss Paget, and see for yourself."

His words were spoken in the same light indifferent tone, but suddenly, for no comprehensible reason, Julia's nervousness, the uncertainty she had felt while waiting in the gloomy hotel, had come back. Her intense excitement, like a potent drink, had worn off, and she felt small, alone, and very cold. This man would tell her nothing, and all the time the wet shining road was taking her nearer to the house that contained a man whose face had changed so that she might not recognise it. And not recognising it, she might find that she was no longer in love.

He had noticed her shivering.

"Are you cold? You'd better put my coat on."

"I'm all right."

"Nonsense. It will get colder all the time. We're getting near the snowline. Like to get out and have a look?"

He stopped the car, and unwillingly she climbed out. The moon was rising, and low hills lay in a long series of black humps against a white background that was not sky but the snow line of the Alps. A chilling wind that seemed to taste of snow and ice blew against her face. Tussocks rustled on the hillside with an incomparably lonely sound. There was the occasional high quavering bleat of a lamb, a lost and eerie sound.

With an almost desperate effort Julia thought of her wedding dress, packed carefully in the bag in the back of the car. But now its snowy folds seemed to her like those mountain peaks, pure and infinitely cold. Her shivering became uncontrollable.

"I hate it!" she muttered. "It's primeval."

The wind tossed the words from her mouth, and she didn't think he heard them. In a moment she was glad. It was betraying her nervousness, and that she never did. She was proud. She accepted adventure.

She felt a coat being flung round her shoulders.

"Put that on," Davey Macauley said crisply.

She clutched at it and scrambled back into the lighted car. In that moment he, and the warmth of the coat, were the only things she had in that lonely spot. She looked at him as he followed her in, seeing him for the first time, the dark hair slicked down, the ears that stuck out like a schoolboy's, the flat mouth drawn down at the corners, the slanted eyebrows and long thin nose. He caught her glance. For a moment the sardonic almost contemptuous humour shone in his eyes. Then he switched off the dashboard light.

"Come along then, Queen of Sheba."

For the rest of that long journey up and down hills, round horseshoe curves, past the steely glimmer of a lake and the pencilled shape of poplars, through the untidy overflow of swollen streams, always towards the white mountains, she remained silent, beyond an occasional question as to how far they still had to go. At last Davey turned the car down a rough road, little more than a track climbing across a hillside.

"We'll be there in ten minutes," he said. "It's just on midnight. You'll see the house round this bend."

Julia could see nothing but what looked like a plantation of trees. Presently they were driving beneath them, the overhanging branches swinging against the car. Julia recognised oak and elm and the flickering white leaves of silver poplar. There was a small grove of pointed Christmas tree firs. Then suddenly, while still in the midst of the trees, they were at the front door of the house. It literally grew among the greenery, a large old wooden two-storey building with two rather pretentious pillars supporting a wide verandah.

Davey stopped the car and Julia slowly climbed out. Instantly the wind seized her and nearly blew her off her feet. The air was full of the creaking and sighing of trees. She had a feeling of being imprisoned in a dark and stormy forest. She stared speechlessly at the house. Perhaps it was only the dim light that made it look so old and tumbledown, so forgotten among all this sad sighing greenery. Paul had written, "Mother wants the house dressed up," but how had they come to let it get into such a dilapidated state? If it had not been for the faint yellow light in one of the upper windows she would not have believed that anyone lived here. Even as she looked a hand—was it a hand, it looked so thin and fleshless?—was silhouetted a moment against the pane, then the blind was pulled down and even that faint light vanished.

Julia became aware that Davey was standing beside her.

"You go in," he said briskly. "The door won't be locked. Just give a shout."

A shout! In that black deserted place? She would never be able to produce more than a quaver of sound.

"Who—will wake up?" she said uncertainly. (The owner of that ghostly hand? Never could she believe that Paul, the blue-eyed healthy normal person she had known, was within these walls.)

"Mrs. Blaine, I should think. Paul's mother. I'll bring your bags in."

Julia gave a swift glance at her stacked luggage in the back of the car. Now she understood Davey's expression as he had looked at it in Timaru. All those elaborate clothes were ludicrous in this wild forsaken place.

"Just give me that little bag," she said swiftly. "That's all I want tonight."

"Sure?" His voice indicated his disbelief that she could do with so little.

"Of course I'm sure," she snapped. Her momentary anger at his impertinence jerked her back into reality, and she was able to walk up the steps on to the porch, and then to turn the knob of the heavy door and open it slowly.

The hall in which she found herself was in darkness except for a slip of light from a room at the far end. She gave a rather tremulous "Yoo hoo!" Then suddenly she seemed to awake at last to the fact that here she was at last under the same roof as Paul. In another moment, provided she could make someone hear, she would be taken to his bedside, she could be face to face with him, the man with whom she had only completely fallen in love after he had written her that tender sensitive letter. In an excess of excitement she ran stumblingly across the hall, which had a faint smell of old dusty carpet, towards the door through which the chink of light showed.

She pushed open the door boldly and there, by a dying fire, was Paul. Of course it was Paul. The room was lit only by two candles on the mantelpiece and the glow of embers from the fire, but there distinctly was his fair head leaning against the back of his armchair, his injured foot resting on a stool.

She tried to speak, but couldn't. She could only draw her breath in in a long audible sigh of excitement.

The sound made him turn his head. He saw her standing in the doorway, and he swung round sharply, his blue eyes, Paul's familiar blue eyes full of astonishment. Then he spoke. "And who the devil are you?" he said.

# FOUR

IT was the dim wavering light, of course. That, and because he hadn't expected her to arrive that night. In a moment Julia had recovered from the shock of his words and had run forward.

"Paul, it's me! Don't you recognise me? But of course you do. Come and look at me under the light. Have I changed so much?"

She was chattering, as she had chattered with Davey in the car. Excitement and uneasiness made her twitter like a disturbed starling. Suddenly she realised she still had on Davey's coat, a heavy camelhair duffel coat with a hood over her head. No wonder Paul didn't recognise her when she was practically obliterated with woolly material. She pushed back the hood and began to laugh merrily. Because in none of her imagined versions of their meeting had there ever been one where Paul didn't recognise her.

Paul picked up his stick and came painfully towards her. Now she was staring at him, thinking that it was the pain of his ankle that made his face look different. Or the shadows made by the flickering candlelight. No, of course not, it was that new nose which seemed to have very slightly altered the shape of his mouth, making it pulled up at the corners instead of firm and easy laughing mouth that she didn't remember. But his blue eyes and his fresh rather florid colouring were the same, also the neat clipped golden moustache that had always seemed something of an affectation in a simple person like Paul.

"Why, you're a pretty thing," he said, as if her looks were quite unexpected.

She was conscious of the faintest surprise. Hadn't he always thought she was pretty?

"Have I changed?" she asked.

For answer he dropped his stick and put his arms round her hard. She was agreeably conscious of the bright ardent look in his eyes, then of his mouth, still disturbingly un familiar, on hers. His kiss was very complete and accom plished. The thought flashed through her head that the Paul she had known had not learnt how to kiss like that. What had been happening during those three silent years? Then she thought fleetingly of her own flirtations, and sur rendered herself to the feel of his lips.

"Why wouldn't you marry me in Wellington?" he de manded.

"But, Paul!" She drew back. "It was too soon. I wanted to see you first. I had to get to know you again."

"Scared, eh?"

"No, of course not. But I only knew you for a few days, and after three years——"

He kissed her again, in that warm expert way, and once more she was conscious of delight, with that faint under current of uneasiness.

He seemed uncannily to sense her uneasiness, for he said, "You don't like my face!"

"But, darling, it's no different."

"Yes, it is. Look!"

He picked up a candle and held it dramatically a few inches from his face.

"See!" he said. "Scars here." He ran his fingers down the faint lines on either side of his nose. "My nose is a different shape. Better, perhaps. I even think I may be more hand some. But not the Paul you remember?"

The last was a question to which he awaited her reply with apparent anxiety.

"No-o," she said slowly. "Not quite. It's not your nose. It's your mouth, I think. Your expression."

"You don't like it?"

"Oh, Paul, of course I do."

He smiled, with that indefinable difference that both pleased and disturbed her.

"That's a tremendous relief. I'd been a bit morbid about the whole thing, I can tell you." Then for the first he seemed to realise her unorthodox arrival. "But why didn't you stay in Timaru as I told you to?"

"Then you did write that letter?"

"Now who else did you think would have written it?"

Again uneasiness stirred in her.

"I don't know. But it wasn't a bit like you. So cold. As if you didn't want me."

"Want you! Don't be a little idiot. But we had quite a night here last night, and then I got this infernal twisted ankle. And all the lights had gone. Perhaps I was a bit curt in that note. I didn't realise it. I'm sorry. But you can see that at present this is no place to bring a girl."

For the first time she looked round the dimly lit room. It was obviously a library, but the books on the shelves looked as if they had not been taken down or dusted for a very long time. There was the cleared place in the centre of the room where Paul had been sitting, a round table, a chair and a faded rug on the floor, but for the rest the piles of newspapers and old magazines, like sand dunes in the wind, were gradually encroaching over the whole of the floor. It looked like a room that had been shut up for a long time. Probably that was what had happened, and now Paul was planning to bring it back into use.

He was watching her. "You're looking at the dust," he said. "You can see how much I need a wife." He gave his unfamiliar smile and lightly ran his hand down her body over the curve of her hips.

Instinctively she drew back. "Don't do that," she said.

His eyebrows went up teasingly. She coloured and said ineptly, "You wouldn't have, once."

"Ah, but we weren't about to be married once. And you've grown so utterly beautiful."

There was a low whistling in the hall, then several thumps. Someone began to sing softly, *"Do not trust him, gentle maiden. . . ."*

Paul seized his stick and limped to the door.

"Davey! What the hell are you doing? What's all that stuff?"

"It's the luggage."

"Julia's?"

Julia went to the door.

"Paul, it's my trousseau."

Paul looked at the small mountain of bags in the hall.

27

"Why, you little plutocrat."

"I didn't buy it. Uncle Jonathan did. It was his wedding present to me."

Then again she was thinking of the immaculate perfection of her wedding dress. Her gaze wandered to the shadowed ceiling. She was almost certain that spider webs hung there. This great sprawling house was full of dust and shadows. She felt as if she were in a dream that was half delicious, half nightmare.

"Now do you see why I wanted you to wait in Timaru?" Paul muttered. "Coming to this old place like a princess. Wait here while I go and wake my mother."

He picked up a candle and limped to the stairs. His shadow preceded him up the wall, flickering and shapeless. It seemed to dance in Julia's brain, like a monstrous moth, and suddenly all her confidence left her. Paul was disturbed by her arrival. For all the smile in his familiar blue eyes she had been aware of the speculation behind it. Something was wrong. She had walked on to the stage without her cue.

She sat on one of the smart labelled bags and put her head in her hands.

"I wish I hadn't come," she whispered involuntarily.

"The trouble with you," came Davey Macauley's dry voice, "is that you're hungry."

Julia looked up sharply. She had forgotten he was there. "Why didn't you tell me it was like this?"

"You insisted on coming to see for yourself."

"But it will be all right," she said, almost in a panic.

"In this life," he said in his offhand way, "being too sensitive isn't amusing. Would you like bacon and eggs?"

His prosaic voice made the fluttering in her head cease.

"Oh, Davey, that would be wonderful."

He disappeared down a dark passage. Before Julia could ponder on the improbability of the shepherd cooking her a meal there was a quick patter of footsteps overhead, and a little plump woman in a flying negligée came down the stairs.

"Julia! My dear child! My dear, dear child! You naughty little creature, taking us by surprise like this."

Julia, getting to her feet, was enveloped in a soft perfumed mass of satin and plump flesh. The lilting voice enveloped her, too.

"We wanted to have everything beautiful for you. That was why Paul so hoped you would spend your honeymoon in the North Island. I was going to work like a beaver while you were away getting this ghastly old house tidied up. But never mind, probably you would like to choose your own furnishings, anyway. So perhaps it's all for the best. Do you find it terribly shocking, arriving by candlelight?"

Julia had a queer feeling that this woman, Paul's mother, so extremely feminine, carrying with her an aura of expensive hotels and sophisticated parties, so unexpectedly in this old dark house, was also trying to hide uneasiness.

"My arrival is the last straw," she said.

"Don't be silly, my dear. Paul is delighted you have come. He says you're astonishingly pretty. Let me look."

Again a candle was raised, this time the flickering flame glowing in Julia's tired eyes and dazzling her.

"My dear," she heard the voice of the little plump woman saying with sudden solicitude, "you look cold!"

That was what was wrong, of course. She was cold and hungry. She had thrown off Davey's duffel coat so that Paul would recognise her, and now suddenly she badly wanted it back on. She was not out in the wind, but she could hear it against the walls and it made her shiver again. This, she thought, was exactly the kind of house where anonymous notes would be pushed under doors, notes saying *You are deliberately running into danger*. If she had on Davey's duffel coat she could stop shivering.

"Julia, this, as you will have gathered, is my mother," she heard Paul saying belatedly, as he limped towards them.

"You must call me Kate," said the woman affectionately. "I *do* hope you will like me, dear. Such a tragedy, when one has a horrid mother-in-law."

Her mouth, thin at the corners, blossomed into fullness in the centre, like a bursting poppy bud, her eyes were small and bright and sharp. She had a large quantity of blonde hair that rippled in innumerable curls. She was an entirely unexpected person. It would not be impossible to imagine

29

her slipping, as a dramatic touch, an anonymous letter under a door.

The thought drifted in and out of Julia's head. She smiled and murmured, "I'm so glad to meet you. You must think I'm crazy bringing all this luggage, but Uncle Jonathan——"

"My dear, it's enchanting. We'll be able to have the sweetest wedding. I adore weddings. I was going to be devastated if Paul had persuaded you to marry him in a registry office. He was just so impatient. But of course one doesn't blame him, after all this time. He's been through such a lot, poor darling."

"Mother!" said Paul deprecatingly, "Julia has already looked at my face. She likes it—a little, I think."

His eyes were on her. She tried to read them. But it was too dark. All she could think of was his hand on her, familiarly. She wished that that hadn't happened, not because she objected so much to it but because it perplexed her. Had she known Paul so little in England? Or had he changed so much? If she had kept Davey's shapeless duffel coat on he wouldn't have had that impulse to touch her.

"Food's ready," came Davey's voice from the kitchen.

"What, haven't you had a meal?" Kate asked.

"But I told Davey to take you to dinner," Paul said.

"We didn't want to waste time," Julia told them. "It was my fault."

"But you must be *expiring!*" Kate cried. "You go and eat while I get your room ready. Then you'll want to go straight to bed."

The food was set on the end of a large table in the kitchen. There was a pleasant smell of frying bacon and woodsmoke. Mercurially Julia felt her spirits rising. She noticed that Davey, the extraordinary fellow, had laid a clean cloth and set the cutlery with some care. This room, an old-fashioned farmhouse kitchen with a high smoke-blackened ceiling and enormous coal range, had a lived-in appearance, and was not so derelict as the rest of the house.

"Lily, our maid, has been away for a week," she heard Kate explaining. "We'd only just got her, and then her mother was ill in Timaru—or so Lily said, so I had to let her go. But she'll be back tomorrow, and we can really get organised. Isn't Davey a treasure?"

"I thought he was a shepherd," Julia murmured, her eyes on Davey's back as he bent silently over the stove.

"Oh, he's one of the family, too. Actually, he's a dark horse. He's writing a book. Paul and he became friends in the North Island, and as he was looking for a job in the country, Paul brought him back. Paul, should you be standing so much on that ankle? When was it last bathed?"

"Mrs. Robinson did it this evening. She'll do it again in the morning. It's all right. Don't fuss, Mother."

"I'm not fussing, darling. I'm just running along to get Julia's room ready. Then perhaps Davey will carry up the bags."

Julia watched for the flash of contempt in Davey's eyes. But Paul intercepted her glance, and gave her a warm secret look that demanded recognition. She smiled back, for one thing at least was eased in her mind. He had not handed her carelessly to his shepherd to look after, he had known that Davey Macauley was a man of superiority and intelligence. That much was explained. For the rest— was she more than a little excited at the thought of his mouth on hers again?

But after the meal Julia was too sleepy to be kissed. She brushed Paul's lips with hers, then stumbled up the stairs after Kate's little bustling figure. She was almost too sleepy to notice that the room into which Kate led her, was crowded with furniture, so that there was scarcely room for the enormous four-poster bed in the centre. There was everything imaginable, carved chests, tasselled footstools, large dark paintings, a chandelier that tinkled softly in the draught that came from the ill-fitting windows, tarnished mirrors, a wardrobe that could easily house several people. A light film of dust lay on everything.

"You see," said Kate apologetically, running her finger over the dressing-table and frowning fastidiously, "how unprepared we were for you. The dust! I'm overcome with shame. But the bed, I know, is comfortable. This, of course, will be Paul's and your room, so now you will be able to plan it yourself. It has a beautiful view of the mountains." She perched on the edge of the bed, her short legs dangling.

"I do hope we shall be friends, Julia dear. It's doubly important to me since Paul is my only son. You've no idea how desperately he counted on his last operation being a success so that he could send for you. He said you were much too sensitive to be tied to a badly scarred man." She sighed deeply. "But now everything is all right. In a few days we'll have the house cleaned up. I can see you're wondering why it's in this dreadful state. I've only just come here, you know. Paul had been away at the war and then he was in hospital. He hasn't been here long, either. Before that there was only Granny who is much too old to notice anything, and a dreadful old couple called Bates whom we had to get rid of at once. The place had gone to rack and ruin."

"Granny?" said Julia. "You mean Georgina Heriot?"

"Georgina Blaine. My late husband's mother. Poor little soul, she's very frail. Paul or Davey carries her up and downstairs. You'll meet her tomorrow, but don't be upset if she doesn't know who you are. Her memory has gone. Now I won't chatter any more because you're asleep on your feet. Goodnight, dear child. And don't get up in the morning. I shall bring you your breakfast myself."

When she had gone, closing the door behind her, Julia could hear only the wind. It breathed heavily against the house, and forced itself through cracks in the window frames, so that the blinds moved in and out with a hooshing sound. The two candles set on the dressing-table wavered constantly.

Julia sat on the edge of the big bed where Kate had sat, and tried to think over the events of the day. She had had another of those stupid poison-pen letters, she had thought Paul had deserted her in Timaru, she had been cold and Davey had lent her his coat, Paul hadn't recognised her in the enveloping coat in the dim light. Kate, in her satin nightdress and negligée, with her perfumed skin and waved hair, had been incongruous in the old dusty house, like a butterfly in a spider's web. Paul had kissed her in a new way. . . .

Julia's lips softened as she thought of that kiss, and the tension went out of her. Someone had brought up her overnight bag and the bag that contained her wedding dress. It

32

could have been no one but Davey, for only he knew about the wedding dress. (Was he being sympathetic at last?) She picked up the bag and opened it and took out the dress. Somehow it was her talisman. She could not bring herself to hang it in the dark cavernous wardrobe which looked as if it might hold spiders or moths, each equally repulsive to Julia, so she spread it over a chair, and she could see it glimmering there even after she had blown out the candles and was lying warmly in the enormous bed.

The house was dreadful, but it would be fun replanning it. She was glad she had come before it was done. This room she would have in yellow and white, because with all those trees shading the house one had to bring in an illusion of sunlight. It would be hers and Paul's room, she thought, as she drifted into sleep. . . .

She wasn't quite sure whether she heard the voices outside or not, the fearful one that said, "Whatever was Davey up to, bringing her out like that? What are we going to *do?*"

It was Kate speaking, although Julia had not heard her use that tone before. She knew that Paul answered, although he only made a "S-s-sh!" and then said something inaudible.

There was a tiny nervous ripple of laughter, then Kate spoke again. "Yes, I agree. She has a charming face. We could have had a *beautiful* wedding."

There was the sound of tiptoeing feet. Without seeing anything, Julia knew that Paul had led his mother, with her anxious questioning, farther along the passage, out of her possible earshot.

It was much later that the fingers touched her face. She had been asleep and she thought it was part of a dream that the scrabbling tree branches outside had got into the room and were moving over her face. Then she became aware of breathing and she started up in the darkness, repressing a scream. The fingers, with their feel of dry twigs, drew sharply back. A voice whispered caressingly, "Harry's wife! I'm so pleased you have come."

"Who is it?" Julia could scarcely make the words audible.

But they were audible enough for her visitor to shuffle backwards quickly. Julia groped for matches. She found

33

them at last and struck one. Instantly the draught from the ill-fitting windows blew it out. She had caught no more than a glimpse of the tiny dark figure that went out at the door.

She knew who it was, of course. It was the owner of that fleshless hand she had seen momentarily silhouetted against the window as she had arrived.

# FIVE

IT was cheap melodrama, of a piece with the anonymous letters, she thought, and awoke for the second time to find that it was daylight and Paul, in his dressing gown, was sitting on her bed. She had the feeling that he had been there for a long time, and that he had been staring at her. For although he was smiling, his mouth soft and easy beneath the faintly golden moustache, there was still speculation in his eyes.

She sat up.

"Paul, who's Harry?"

His smile stiffened. Did he hesitate for the merest second?

"Harry was my brother. He died of pneumonia in Australia."

"Oh, Paul, I'm sorry."

"It was a great blow to my mother. He was only twenty-six, and he was her favourite son. She likes cities and lots of people and things happening, and so did Harry. If he were alive she would never have come to this place, as you can imagine."

Julia thought of Kate's fussy, feminine night things, and golden curls and perfume, so incongruous in this old tumble-down place. She was relieved by the simple explanation. She hadn't realised that Kate's out-of-character appearance had nagged at her so much as those silly letters she had been getting.

"She came when she heard about you," Paul went on. "She knew you would feel strange coming to such a lonely place after a city life, and of course she was longing for a pretty daughter-in-law anyway."

"That's very kind of her," Julia murmured.

"Oh, we're all kind people," said Paul lightly. He leaned towards her. She anticipated the feel of his lips and her blood began to stir. But suddenly he drew back.

"What made you ask about Harry?"

Some instinct made her hesitate to tell him. She had a queer feeling that she had to protect that strange little figure who had crept into her room last night. And what did she know of Paul, really? Had she learned that she could trust him?

For heaven's sake! she thought impatiently. Paul's the man I'm going to marry. Of course I trust him. Of course I shall have no secrets from him, except perhaps about those letters, which might hurt and upset him.

"Someone came into my room last night and touched me and said 'Harry's wife,' " she told him. "When I tried to light the candle she went away."

"Oh, that would be Granny. She must have heard your arrival. She's quite senile, poor old thing. I'm sorry you were frightened, darling."

"I wasn't frightened," said Julia calmly. "But why did she say 'Harry's wife'?"

"For some reason she's got it in her head that Harry is in the house. She's been like that ever since she was told that he had died. The extraordinary thing is that he scarcely ever came here, anyway. But he was rather a charmer, that lad. Women remembered him. The old girl said he took after her."

"She must have had her points," Julia said. "There's my Uncle Jonathan who isn't a woman hater by any means, but he's been faithful to her all his life." Then she said softly, "Poor Paul."

He looked at her questioningly.

"It can't have been much fun having a brother whom everyone petted."

His eyes twinkled with their confident mirth.

"I got by," he said.

"I'm sure you did."

The funny thing was that Paul had not had this confidence three years ago. Then his shy behaviour could have been that of someone who had been ignored for a more amusing and charming brother. Had Harry's death given him the assurance he had lacked? That was not altogether a happy thought. More likely it was the maturing experience of the war.

But Julia had no time to be introspective about it, for now Paul's arms were under her shoulders and he was kissing her very completely.

"Do you love me?" he demanded.

She nodded, her lips still held beneath his.

"You're not going to let my brother's ghost come between us?"

"Paul, how absurd! I didn't even know you had a brother."

He laughed, with a reckless air.

"It's me, and me alone?"

"Paul, you are so silly. Of course it's you alone."

"How long have you loved me?"

She considered. "Well—a little that week we met, but you hardly ever wrote and I thought you had forgotten me. Uncle Jonathan used to say, 'Haven't you heard from that scallawag?' Then"—her voice softened—"there was that absolutely wonderful letter you wrote me saying all those things."

"It was rather a good letter, wasn't it," he said smugly.

"Oh, Paul, don't tease. If you do I'll think you didn't mean the things you said in it."

"You sentimental little goat! Falling in love with a letter. You know that I would have written long ago if it hadn't been for my face." He kissed her again, and this time his fingers were fumbling against her breast. As last night when he had become too intimate Julia felt a tremor of distaste running through her. Was she a prude, she wondered uneasily. She loved Paul, soon she would be his wife, surely this slight familiarity was not objectionable. It couldn't be that she disliked his touch. . . . She gently drew away from him, but made herself touch the scar running parallel with his nose, the nose she didn't quite know. Or was it the mouth, untouched, uninjured, that she had least recognised? It was because this was a Paul she didn't entirely know that the feel of his hands made her sensitive. In a day or two she would be at ease with him. For she understood completely what had happened. Not only had he had an injured face, but he had an inferiority complex induced by a younger and more popular brother. He had had to get one mended and the other out of his system. Now he was a different person, whole and sane and uninhibited. And after all wasn't he the person who had written that beautiful tender letter?

"Well, you two lovebirds," came Kate's gay voice from the doorway. She was still in the peach-coloured satin negligée, and she carried a tray. She looked older by daylight, her little full-blown mouth at variance with the deep lines on either side of it, her hair a too-improbably pale gold.

"Julia, darling, you must be starving. I hope you like eggs for breakfast. Lily will be back later this morning, and then you can have what you please, but I find boiling an egg absolutely all I can do first thing in the morning. Now Paul, get off the bed and let me put this tray down. My God, isn't this room a mausoleum! I think Julia is extremely charitable even to sleep in it."

"Serves her right for barging in like that last night," Paul said unsympathetically.

"Darling, how rude you are! Isn't he, Julia? Personally I think it was tremendous fun having her arrive like that. Paul, should you be on that ankle?"

"It's much better this morning, Mother. Mrs. Robinson is going to fix it later."

"Is she? Julia, I'm warning you, you'll have to watch this man. The women fall over themselves to do things for him. Mrs. Robinson will walk miles to put a bandage on his little finger, and as for Lily, she just goes gooey-eyed the moment he appears."

Lily, Julia thought rapidly, had been away for a week because her mother had been ill. She could have been in Wellington two days ago, and in Timaru yesterday. Was she the poison-pen person? And who was Mrs. Robinson?

Paul grinned, his eyes almost wickedly confident.

"Julia will take care of all that, Mother."

37

"Will I?" Julia murmured. Would she have liked him to be just a little less assured? But when he was used to his newly acquired confidence he would settle down to a more balanced state.

Before she went downstairs she began a letter to Uncle Jonathan.

"I am here, Uncle darling. I am so excited——" she hesitated. Then she wrote firmly, "——and happy. Paul is the same, yet different, excitingly different, and as he seems to be a popular young man among the women I shall have to watch myself to see that I do not become a jealous wife. His mother is a dear, too. She is tremendously interested in my beautiful trousseau——"

Julia paused again, remembering Kate opening the door of the wardrobe and then standing staring, her little ripe-plum mouth falling open with an expression that seemed to be not only admiration but dismay.

—and the sight of my wedding dress left her speechless. I am afraid I have upset their plans, as Paul wanted to be married quietly in Wellington as soon as I arrived, and Kate was going to have the house here renovated while we were on our honeymoon. I must admit I can't help wondering why something wasn't done about the house sooner, as they have known for three months that I was coming. However, it is rather fun seeing it in its original state, with all the furniture Georgina and Adam Blaine had. My room has a window that opens on to a balcony, and when I stand out there I can see through a gap in the trees all the way to the Southern Alps. The mountain air is icy, but all the same I shall go out on my balcony every morning and breathe it in until I get used to it. The climate in the South of France has made me soft. This house is in a very isolated position, and they say if there is a bad snowstorm it is quite cut off. . . .

Julia stopped there, thinking of what it would be like to be shut up here alone with Paul. She threw down her pen, because suddenly she had an imperative desire to see Paul again. She had lingered long enough upstairs, anyway. The morning was slipping away, and there was still all the house to see.

She ran downstairs, then hesitated in the hall wondering where to look for Paul. He would not be far away, with that bad ankle. She was going to look in the library where she had found him last night when voices coming from the direction of the kitchen arrested her.

There was a woman laughing. There was Paul's voice, and then the woman laughing again.

"Oh, go on with you!" Julia heard her say.

"My little dove!"

Dove! thought Julia indignantly. Dove, indeed! Here, probably, was the author of those stupid anonymous letters, here was the jealous woman who was afraid of losing Paul.

But she would play fair. She strolled casually towards the kitchen, humming.

The voices stopped. Paul called, "Is that you, Julia? Come and meet my nurse."

In the kitchen Paul was sitting on a low chair with his leg outstretched. The bandage was off his ankle, and a buxom red-headed woman with sparkling green eyes was bathing the inflamed flesh.

Paul said, "This is Mrs. Robinson, Julia. She has the quite absurd name of Dove."

"I think it's delightful," Julia said, suddenly wanting to laugh with relief at the very simple explanation for Paul's overheard words. (But had he needed to speak in that caressing voice?) "How useful that you know how to treat a sprain, Mrs. Robinson."

The woman had her head bent now. Julia's eyes rested on her fiery mass of hair that was confined with a violet-coloured ribbon.

"I used to be a nurse," she said briefly.

"And that's a very valuable accomplishment in the country," Paul said. "If ever your husband wants to leave, Dove, we shall certainly bribe you to stay."

The woman flashed him a swift emerald glance. Then she quickly and capably wrapped a bandage round Paul's ankle and said, "There! That will be all right, Mr. Blaine. But for goodness' sake keep off that foot. You'll have the swelling twice as bad again."

Paul looked at Julia. It seemed to her, suddenly that his face was a choir-boy's, full of what was at once innocence and guile.

"You must stop these women hen-pecking me, Julia. Lily does it, too. I get no peace at all."

Dove Robinson imperturbably picked up the basin of water.

"I'll be going now. I'll come over again this evening."

As she went out, her burning head held high, Julia said involuntarily, "I believe she's jealous."

Paul smiled lazily.

"And why not? You're so charming."

"But it's ridiculous. She has a husband, hasn't she?"

"A dull sort of a fellow, scarcely knows a woman from a sheep."

"So you comfort her by calling her your little Dove."

Paul began to laugh.

"My darling, I believe it's you who are jealous."

"Well, what do you think? I don't believe in sharing my husband with every discontented woman he meets. Besides——"

But Paul had come to her and was kissing her so that she could not say what she had been going to about those childish letters. And, anyway, wasn't it better not to talk about them, silly mischief-making articles that they were. Now she thought, it could well be fiery-headed Dove Robinson who had written them and arranged with someone in Wellington and Timaru to deliver them. Well, Dove could soon be dealt with. She was not afraid of a woman.

"Close your eyes," said Paul's voice in her ear. "The perfect kiss is always made with closed eyes."

"Paul when did you become such a connoisseur in this art——" Julia was interrupted by a sudden sharp thumping on the ceiling overhead. She drew back. "What's that?"

Paul sighed. "Oh, that's Granny. She wants to come down. Davey must do it while I have this bad ankle.

Sweet, do you mind calling Davey. He'll be out at the back somewhere, or in the cottage in the orchard. And of course you must meet Granny. But I warn you, she'll talk a lot of pathetic nonsense, poor little soul. She won't really know who you are. Do you mind coming to such a peculiar household, my love?"

His words were humble, but his gaze was not. It had that mixture of innocence and boldness that she was beginning to find acutely disturbing. It had almost the same effect as his too-familiar hands on her body. She felt it like a caress.

"I'll go for Davey," she said hurriedly, but even as she went she thought sensibly, "I can't run away from the way he looks at me, and the way he touches me all the time. The only thing to do is to like it."

A track ran from the back door beneath the heavily arching trees through a sagging wooden gate and across the damp grass of the orchard. It led to a sloping-roofed cottage with a wooden verandah, and the front door standing open. Julia tapped at the door and waited. There was no answer. "Davey!" she called. "Are you there?"

The door that stood open led straight into the living room. It was dominated by a writing desk under the window that was covered with writing materials in fantastic disarray. Julia's fingers itched to tidy it, then she shrugged her shoulders fatalistically. Tidying up at Heriot Hills was going to be a long job. It was hardly seemly that she start with the shepherd's cottage.

She went into the room, however, and stood idly pressing the rocker of the ancient rocking chair as she gazed at a picture hanging above the mantelpiece. It was a Venetian scene, and it had the dusty sunlit effect of a Canaletto. Probably a reproduction, Julia thought idly, and was startled from her thoughts by Davey's voice.

"What do you want? Your bags carried up?"

She turned sharply to see him in the doorway, dressed in plaid shirt, corduroy trousers, and riding boots. A picturesque shepherd, she thought lightly, the kind that Texas would call a tenderfoot.

"Davey, can't you stop harping on my bags," she said

41

pleasantly. "It's old Mrs. Blaine who wants to be brought down. Will you come now? I'm longing to meet her."

"All right," he said. Then he added casually, "Have a good night?"

"Why not?" Suddenly she said, "Did you know Paul's brother, Harry?"

"No. Have you met him already?" He was watching her, his eyes full of interest. She couldn't think what had made her ask him that question. Of course he could not have known Paul's brother who had died in Australia some time ago.

"How could I when he is dead? You know he was dead," she accused.

"Perhaps I meant his ghost," he said lightly. "The old lady thinks it is in the house. She's astonishingly emphatic about it."

"So Paul says," Julia said uneasily. "But she's a little senile."

"Just the sort of person to converse with a ghost. Well, let's go, shall we?"

She cast a quick look round the room. She sighed.

"I like this. It's so beautifully uncluttered, except for your desk, of course. Are you really writing a book?"

"Do you think it is a disguise for a more sinister occupation?"

His dark unreadable eyes teased her. Then he took her elbow and guided her to the door. In that instant the feeling she had had when his warm coat had protected her from the sweeping snowy wind last night came back to her. She felt enclosed in a small circle of warmth. It was an odd feeling, disturbing in its way, but completely unrelated to the excitement that overcame her when Paul kissed her. She moved quickly away from him and said,

"It really was a wise thing coming last night. Paul is delighted. So is his mother. It was only that they were worried about the state of the house, but it will be fun fixing it. I have all sorts of ideas."

"I am sure you have. Who will you get to do the interior decorations. Marcus Blount?" He mentioned a well-known decorator.

"That isn't very funny," said Julia. "Just because I have

a Lanvin dress through no fault of my own. Anyway, you have a Canaletto."

"A copy," he said quickly.

She looked at him. He had spoken too quickly. His narrow brown face gave nothing at all away, yet in that moment she knew that the little dusty golden picture over the fireplace in the shepherd's cottage was a genuine Canaletto. She knew it without a shadow of doubt.

Who was he? What was he?

He went on talking, again too quickly, making her think of her own unease when she chattered.

"In the midst of this redecorating and marrying you might just remind your husband that there are sheep on his property and the lambing season is beginning."

Into Julia's mind there flashed the small intimate picture of Paul lounging in the low chair while the voluptuous Dove bent over his injured ankle. Again her defences were down.

"But he always used to talk as if he had no interest but his farm."

"Perhaps he's a little out of practice," Davey commented drily. "From what I can see the farm is in much the same state as the house. It's a pity."

"Then Paul and I must go into that. He's been in hospital so much, that's what the trouble is. He's had no time to attend to work. Hasn't he told you that?"

Davey went ahead of her to open the rickety gate that led up to the house.

"Just as a matter of interest," he said, "do you know how long scarring from a skin graft takes to fade?"

They were at the back door, and there was no more to be said. Davey went inside and up the stairs with his long light stride, and Julia, waiting, wondering whether to think Davey's remark insolence or not, thought, "If the operation were recent the scars would be much more vivid. Of course I know that. Paul's scars are scarcely visible. They must have been made a year, perhaps more than a year, ago. Why has Kate lied about it, and Paul too? Why all this lapse of time before he wrote to me? That's what Davey is trying to tell me."

# SIX

THE old lady was exactly like a white rabbit. When Davey put her down her head emerged from the several shawls she had draped round her tiny shoulders, and there she was with her pale mild eyes, her little sharp nose that twitched constantly at its pink tip, her mass of fluffy white hair. Julia found herself unable to stop staring. So this, she thought, this quaint miniature morsel who snuffed faintly as she breathed, was the person Uncle Jonathan had treasured in his memory for so many years. She tried to create round the fragile bones the young radiant flesh that Uncle Jonathan remembered. Yes, perhaps she had been a delectable little person, blue-eyed, soft-mouthed, pink of cheek. It was pathetic, shocking, to think that the image Uncle Jonathan carried was in reality this shrunken snuffling little bundle of bones that showed no spark of interest or intelligence.

Julia suddenly wanted to weep, for Uncle Jonathan and his so truly-lost Georgina. It was a mistake to live too long. She and Paul, on the threshold of their life would come to this. She tried to visualize Paul as an ageing man, and failed utterly. He existed only as the virile young man with the innocent choir-boy face whom she knew.

She was aware of Davey looking at her over the old woman's head.

"You knew she was very old," he said.

She was uncomfortably aware that he had read her thoughts.

"Don't let this place make you introspective," he said uncannily, and just as she was thinking that she could imagine Davey growing old, the flesh growing spare over those thin long bones, Kate came bouncing into the room.

"Thank you, Davey, for bringing Granny down. She was

getting impatient." As Davey went out Kate said, "Julia, come and speak to her. I'm afraid she won't have any idea who you are. Granny dear," she bent over the bundle of shawls surmounted by the faintly trembling white head, "this is Julia Paget, the girl Paul is going to marry."

The filmy blue eyes turned on Julia. One hand, the dry twiglike shape that Julia had felt on her cheek in the night, was slightly raised. Julia took it, and she heard the little voice, high, like a sleepy bird's, "So pretty. Now I would like my morning chocolate. Send Mrs. Bates to me, dear."

Kate said quickly in an undertone, "Mrs. Bates isn't here. She and her husband, a dreadful old couple, were here when Paul and I came, and we had to get rid of them. The house is bad enough now, but you should have seen it then, such a mess. But Granny didn't notice, poor soul, and she was used to them."

She raised her voice. "Granny, you know Mrs. Bates isn't here now. Lily is here. She will make your chocolate. She makes it very nicely. You know that."

The old lady's mouth trembled. "I would prefer Mrs. Bates. I'm used to her. I don't like changes." She peered at Kate. "What is your name?"

"Now, Granny! You know very well. I'm Kate, your daughter-in-law."

The old lady stared.

"I don't remember your name. How foolish of me. If you are my daughter-in-law I should know you. But there is so much to remember, so much to forget. I forget the wrong things. Mrs. Bates get so cross with me. Now, she says . . ." The faint voice twittered on. Kate drew Julia away.

"She just does that all day. You can't really talk sense to her. Now, dear, do you see the kind of house we tried to prevent you from coming to. If only Paul had sent for me earlier. I'm so angry with him. Poor child, what do you think of it all?"

"We all come to this," said Julia slowly, looking at the little whittled-down face of Uncle Jonathan's lovely Georgina.

"Now, darling, don't be *morbid!*" Kate cried. "That would be just the last straw. Come out and meet Lily. She's just arrived back. She's a lively young thing who will take your mind off age. We'll all have chocolate. Or a brandy if you

45

prefer it. I always feel I could do with one after a session with Granny. You know, she has her wedding dress ready to be buried in, and she insists on looking at it every day to see that the moths haven't got into it."

Kate looked at Julia and suddenly clapped her hand to her mouth.

"Oh, darling Julia, what an ass I am! When you have that beautiful beautiful dress up there. I just didn't think——"

"Perhaps some day I should like to be buried in it," Julia said dreamily.

"My God, now you are morbid! Come along out of this fusty room."

The room was a large one looking north, and darkened to a green gloom by the overhanging trees. Julia observed the relics of another generation, the spinning wheel, the velvet tasselled overmantel, the pictures of sailing ships coming into the brown and barren-hilled New Zealand harbours, the yellowed keys of the old upright piano, the round-back couches with their worn tapestry covers, the vase of dried and brittle *toi toi* grass, like a plume of biscuit-coloured hair.

As Kate took her out the high piping voice followed them,

"But are you *sure* you want to marry Harry, Julia?"

Kate would not let Julia go back.

"It's quite ridiculous the way she insists Harry is here," she said crossly. "Isn't it bad enough being always reminded that we have lost him?" Her little ripe mouth trembled, and finally it was Julia who had to comfort her and take her out to the kitchen where a blonde-haired girl with a tall supple body was setting cups on a tray.

Julia watched the girl closely as Kate performed introductions. She had narrow rather sly blue eyes and a pasty skin, but her body was lovely. So was her smooth genuinely silver-blonde hair. She hadn't the guile to darken her colourless eyebrows or eyelashes, but even without that she had seductiveness enough. Julia had a feeling of certainty that here was the author of those childish notes. The girl was in love with Paul, her watchful sidelong glances at Julia told that.

The situation was almost humorous. There was the red-headed Dove and the blonde Lily. One needed now only a brunette. Then Paul could be really triumphant over his conquests. Funny shy Paul who had scarcely known even how to kiss her three years ago.

"Where have you been, Lily?" she asked.

"In Timaru." The girl, it was clear, was not going to be over-friendly. Probably, at this moment, she was composing another note, a more strongly-worded one that would do what the previous ones had failed to accomplish.

"Just Timaru?"

The girl gave her a sidelong glance.

"I've been with my mother. She's sick. It wasn't a holiday."

"I'm sure it wasn't," said Kate placatingly. "But I hope you're feeling fit because we're going to have an awfully busy time. The whole house has to be done from top to bottom."

Lily looked at her suspiciously.

"What's going to happen to old Mrs. Blaine?"

"Oh, we'll tuck her away somewhere comfortable. Poor little soul, she won't notice a thing."

Lily muttered something. Kate said in her clear sharp voice,

"What did you say, Lily?"

"I said she notices more than you think, ma'am."

"Oh, I don't think so, Lily. She lives entirely in a make-believe world. Take her the hot chocolate now. That's all she wants for happiness, food and warmth. So simple, isn't it? One almost envies her."

It was later that Julia heard Paul's welcome to Lily.

"Ah, the lily of the field is back. She toils not, neither does she spin."

"Come off it," Lily retorted tartly, but with an undertone of pleasure.

He had them eating out of his hand, Julia thought with mingled admiration and wryness. That made things easy for him, but how did she handle the situation? Well, it might just be amusing. At least, one hoped it would be amusing.

The third woman arrived that night.

It was a confused day, mostly taken up with Kate exclaiming rapturously over the contents of Julia's bags, and threatening with every other breath to call Paul up and show him a nightgown or a negligée or the kind of underwear that the most expensive Parisian shops thought a bride should wear. Yet behind Kate's enthusiasm and her greedy love of pretty clothes Julia thought she could detect uneasiness. Her small bright eyes darted so quickly here and there. Was she thinking about other women and wondering if Julia should be seriously warned about Dove and Lily? Julia contemplated telling her about the letters, then decided to keep her own counsel in the meantime. There was no point in making trouble about a childish prank.

Julia's head began to ache and she longed for fresh air. The faint musty smell of the house, as if it had been shut up for years, combined with Kate's rather overpowering perfume was becoming too much for her. She planned to take a short walk before the clouds, that threatened an early darkness, came down, and the countryside became too sombre and frightening. She wanted to think before she finished the letter to Uncle Jonathan. She was not so sure now about that sentence, "I am so excited and so happy." She wanted to be honest.

She was delayed in leaving the house, however. She could not decide at first whose was the voice that called her, or where it came from. Then she recognised it. Georgina's. The white rabbit with the twittering voice like a sleepy bird's. It came from a room at the end of the passage upstairs. It was surprisingly strong and clear.

"Julia! Is that you? Come here. I want to talk to you."

She had been put back to bed, and now she sat bolt upright in the middle of an enormous four-poster. A bed-jacket of fluffy white wool enhanced her white-rabbit appearance. She looked like a child's toy. But what surprised Julia was that the vague look had gone from her face and it was sharp and alert. Obviously, she was having one of her occasional intelligent periods. She patted the edge of the bed and said,

"Sit down, my dear. On the bed. I'm afraid you won't find an empty chair. I can do nothing myself, and now Mrs. Bates has gone there is no one I can ask to do things.

48

Kate hasn't learned to manage a house this size yet, and that girl in the kitchen can do nothing but flirt."

She smiled as Julia sat down, and her face took on a kind of spectral warmth so that for a moment she was more like a human being.

"Now tell me, how do you like Heriot Hills?"

Julia looked round the gloomy room and hesitated.

"I—I've scarcely decided."

"Of course not. It's all too strange. I remember when I came here. There were no trees at all, only bare hills with those horrid thorny bushes, and patches of snow. I used to hang my crinolines over the gooseberry bushes to save them from the frost. I was very unhappy. I longed to go home." Then she said, "How's Jonathan?"

"He's very frail. He always talks about you."

Again the ghostly smile crept over the tiny old face, there was a flirtatious coyness in the faded eyes.

"Ah! Sentimental Jonathan. I imagine he always hoped I would find I had made a mistake and go back to him. It doesn't pay to be sentimental." Her voice became sharp and querulous. "He ought to have known better. I hope that you will know better. Don't let Harry make you unhappy. He's a bad boy."

Julia leaned forward.

"Mrs. Blaine, it's Paul I am marrying."

The awareness flickered and vanished in the old lady's eyes. They were a cloudy sky without light.

"Why does everyone say Harry isn't here? He is. He came in here last night and talked to me. He said you were the prettiest of them all."

"Of them all?"

"Girls," the old lady twittered. "Harry likes girls."

"So does Paul, I think," Julia murmured.

"But he's slower than Harry. Much slower."

Julia thought of Dove, and sly-eyed Lily. Her bewilderment grew. This Harry must have been some character.

"Paul takes after his father," the old lady said. "Harry takes after me." She chuckled. "The way I twisted poor Jonathan round my little finger. But he was sweet. Tell him I was asking after him."

49

"Mrs. Blaine," Julia said earnestly, "Harry isn't here. You know he isn't here."

A gleam, like the sun through clouds, shone in Georgina's eyes. Then it vanished. She spoke in her high silly bird's voice.

"You all think I'm crazy. But I'm not. You'll meet Harry before long. You won't be able to escape, a pretty girl like you."

Julia gazed pityingly at the vacant face. The image in Uncle Jonathan's mind was the real Georgina. This was just a sad little shadow.

Nevertheless the odd conversation was disturbing. Julia went across the overgrown garden following a track that led beneath the drooping birches and the firs on to the open hillside. Then the mountain wind came pure and cold in her face, and the evening held only the sound of lambs crying and the stirring of the snowgrass in the wind. She climbed to the top of a low hill, and stood looking across the lonely landscape that spread in a shadowy line of hills broken by the smoky blue of a lake, and isolated clumps of trees, to the towering mountains. Looking at the mountains the same intense loneliness that she had felt last night with Davey overcame her. It wasn't so much loneliness as premonition. Those great giants with their snowcaps were waiting, watching, holding their breath over something. Overwhelmingly she thought of her wedding dress hanging in the dark wardrobe, a snow thing like the mountain tops. In it she would feel as cold as snow. As cold as Georgina would be when for the last time she wore the dress she was afraid the moths would ruin. . . .

"Paul!" she whispered pleadingly.

Then the queer dark feeling passed and she was laughing at her fancies. Paul, growing more and more irritable with his helplessness, was in the house waiting for her. She would ask for a fire to be lit in the library, and some comfortable chairs to be taken in. She and Paul could spend their evening there, cosy and undisturbed. The snow mountains could be shut out.

She turned eagerly back to the house.

Paul was in the library with its rows of books that looked as if they hadn't been touched for half a century. He was not alone. Kate was there, too, and Julia had the instant impression that she had interrupted them in a serious conversation. Just for one moment they stared at her wordlessly. Then Kate sprang up.

"Ah, my dear, you've been out in the cold wind. Come and get warm. Paul and I have just been discussing things."

"What things?" Julia enquired politely.

"Oh, the farm. Re-stocking it, it's terribly neglected, as Davey tells us every day. What to do with the house——"

"You," said Paul, his mouth tilted in his silent laughter.

"Me?" The gentle emphasis in Paul's voice made her flush with pleasure.

"And why not, indeed?" said Kate. "You are the most important person at the moment. You have those lovely lovely clothes and they must be shown off. Besides, we have to bring Heriot Hills back to the way it used to be. The Blaines were quite the most important people in this part of the country. But my poor husband died, and I got so lonely here I couldn't stand it. Besides, the boys had to go to school, and then there was the war. And Granny was getting too old to see that the place was managed properly. She had those dreadful Bates people here, as I told you. But now it's all going to be quite different. Paul will have the sweetest little bride, and of course she must have the right setting."

It was clear that Kate was suddenly tremendously enthusiastic and excited about the prospect of restoring Heriot Hills to its correct standing in the country. But why hadn't she been excited yesterday or a week ago, or three months ago when Paul had decided to marry?

"It looks as if I have been on trial," she said lightly.

Kate looked momentarily confused. Then she laughed, her little plump mouth opening vertically.

"I admit I was a nervous mother-in-law. Paul tried to describe you——"

"Mother, stop talking," Paul said lazily. "I'll convince Julia about this."

Kate sprang to her feet playfully. "Ah, I can see you want to get rid of me. Very well, I can take a hint. But don't forget to fix your wedding date, because there's the minister to see and the invitations to get out—oh, all right, I'm going."

She pattered out, her little plump feet very light in her high-heeled shoes. Paul beckoned to Julia and held out his arms.

"Do you want to talk, my sweet? Or just kiss me?"

His eyes had the bright reckless look that both puzzled and pleased her.

"I was a gamble," she said intuitively.

"Stop talking nonsense." He drew her down to him. She felt the softness of his little golden moustache brush her cheek. "When will you marry me?"

She persisted. "But if I was a gamble why did you want to marry me in Wellington the moment I came off the ship?"

"You were only a gamble as far as this place was concerned. We thought you might hate it here. Are you going to hate it?"

His lips pressed on hers. She could only vaguely shake her head, forgetting the wind from the high lonely mountains, the shivering desolation that had filled her.

"Then I'll go to town in a day or two as soon as I can get about on this infernal ankle, and arrange about stock, and then we'll be married. There's a little church overlooking the lake, you stand at the altar and think you're on the lakeside."

"But, Paul!" Something still nagged at her. "If I hadn't liked it here, weren't you going to stay either?"

"Naturally not. Stupid! Do you think you'll like standing at the altar on the edge of a lake?"

Julia nodded happily, thinking that at last everything fell into place. Until now she had not been able to imagine herself really wearing the snowy dress and laying her hand trustingly in Paul's. But now it was going to be true.

"Oh, darling!" she said breathlessly, and at the same moment the doorbell rang with a rusty clangour.

Paul started up impatiently.

"Bother! Who's this?"

"I'll go," said Julia. "You rest that foot, or you won't be able to go and buy Davey's sheep."

"Why Davey's sheep, I'd like to know?"

She turned at the door, laughing. "Poor Davey wants them. How can he be a successful shepherd without them?"

"Then tell him to complain to me!" Paul's voice followed her.

But she laughed again, confidently, thinking it would be fun to tell Davey that it was true, the neglected state of Heriot Hills was going to be remedied very quickly, as she had said it would be.

She pulled open the heavy creaking hall door, and in the gloom on the verandah stood the thin dark-haired girl with the baby in her arms.

Julia drew back a step. The stranger was the first to speak.

"This is Heriot Hills, isn't it? The bus driver told me to come up this road."

"Yes, this is Heriot Hills." (The brunette, Julia was thinking wildly. She had thought about a brunette, and here she stood! It was a dream.)

"Oh, that's all right, then. Lord, it was a hump up that road with my bag and a baby, too. Is"—she hesitated the slightest fraction—"Paul in?"

Julia said uncertainly, "Yes, indeed. Come in. Paul has a bad ankle. I'll call him. But I don't know who you——"

Her sentence was finished by Paul's low exclamation at the end of the hall. "Nita!"

The girl laughed, a slow, amused and yet excited laugh. As she came into the lamplit hall (Kate had discovered an oil lamp and hung it that day) Julia saw that she was good-looking in a thin tense way. She was also well dressed. She must have had quite a time walking up the rough road in those delicate shoes.

"Hullo, Paul," she said. "You see, I came after all. I brought Timmy, too."

Paul limped forward. Whatever he had felt at the evidently unexpected appearance of this girl he played the part of a surprised and genial host very well.

"Why on earth didn't you send a telegram? Davey would at least have met the bus. Walking up that road with a heavy baby! Put him down and come and meet Julia. Julia, this is Nita. Harry's wife."

53

# SEVEN

THAT night, after Julia had gone to bed and put out the light, Paul came into the room and lay on the bed beside her. She could feel the hard ridge on his body through the blankets.

"Paul!" she whispered.

"Be quiet!" he said. He took her in his arms and kissed her until her mouth hurt. She tried to draw away, but the hardness of his grip increased.

"We'll be married quickly," he said.

"But, darling——"

"Now I have my way," he said definitely.

Julia reached out her arm to grope for matches.

"What do you want?"

"I want to light the candle. I want to see you."

"Why?"

"Because you don't sound like yourself. Something has happened. You talk as though if I don't marry you soon you're afraid I never will."

All he answered was, "Nothing's happened. Except Nita coming, of course."

That was it, Julia thought. Nita coming unexpectedly like that with the baby. Paul may have disguised his feelings behind his pleasant affability, but Kate had been unable to hide her agitation. She had put it down to the difficulty of preparing another bedroom in the ramshackle old house and how they were going to cope with the requirements of a fifteen-month-old baby, but her distress was disproportionate. Hadn't she liked her son Harry's wife?

"Paul," Julia said, "why did you tell me Nita was Harry's wife?"

He moved back.

"Because she is."

"No, darling. His widow."

"My God, don't split hairs! You know that was what I meant."

"Yes, of course. I'm sorry. It's just that——"

"Just what?"

Julia thought of Nita's thin face that had a hungry yet excited look. She said slowly,

"She doesn't look like a widow."

"Nita isn't the kind to look sad," Paul said shortly. "She's too tense, too edgy. She'll take it out of herself in other ways, but she won't let you see she's sad."

"We must be kind to her," Julia murmured.

When he didn't answer she finally reached the box of matches and succeeded in striking a match. She held the frail flame up to Paul's face, laughing at him behind it, her tousled hair tumbling into her eyes.

"You're lovely!" he said involuntarily. Then he blew out the match and holding her again in that hard painful embrace muttered, "Let's be married soon. Soon!"

Julia lay stiffly, suddenly deeply glad of the bed coverings between them. For Paul wasn't being kind about Nita. She had seen that in his face as she had held up the match. The laughter had been flattened out of his mouth. It had had an implacable look. For a little while she was not sure that she loved him at all.

After that she couldn't go to sleep. She lay awake listening to the wind that lashed overhanging branches against the house until it seemed that the whole house was rocking and floating in a green sea. Much later, above the sound of the wind, she heard Nita's baby Timmy begin to cry. He had been put to sleep in the little room across the passage from Julia's room, and apparently wherever his mother was she could not hear his cries.

Finally they became so pathetic that Julia got up and went in to him. He was tucked up in an old cradle that no doubt had done service for Georgina's baby sixty years earlier. Timmy was a well-grown little boy, and the cradle was obviously a little too short for him. He had become cramped and uncomfortable, and was protesting emphatically. But when he saw the wavering flame of the candle that Julia held he began to laugh with delight, his flushed chubby face crinkling charmingly. On an impulse Julia put the candle down and gathered him into her arms. He continued to express his appreciation with murmurs of pleasure.

"Where's your mother?" asked Julia. She didn't know where Nita was sleeping, and she shrank from rousing the house. If she was upstairs it was odd that she had not heard Timmy. The window of Timmy's room looked over the back garden and the orchard and the path that led to Davey's cottage. Julia could see a light shining in one of the windows. She looked at her wrist watch and saw that the time was one o'clock. Why was Davey up so late? Suddenly, for no reason at all, the thought came to her that Nita may have been down there. That was why she had not heard Timmy crying. If she had been in the house she must have heard him.

Her suspicions had no foundation. As far as she knew Nita had never seen Davey in her life before. Yet something made her carry Timmy back into her own room and take him into bed with her. He murmured contentedly, his fingers exploring her face. Then he fell asleep, and she put her arm round him protectively and was filled with comfort. The wind had not abated, but now it no longer disturbed her, she no longer imagined she could see it flinging the snow off the high mountains in a white spray. She began to drift into sleep. Even the sound of a girl's laugh, low and satisfied, not very far away, perhaps outside beneath her window, or perhaps on the stairway, didn't deeply penetrate her consciousness.

But in the morning she remembered it. For it was then that she found the letter pushed beneath her door. It was printed in the familiar heavy printing. It read, *Paul Blaine is no good for you. Don't be a fool.*

Julia scarcely had time to thrust the slip of paper into her dressing-gown pocket before Nita burst in.

"Julia, have you got Timmy? Oh, there he is! I got the most terrible fright when I saw his empty cradle."

She swooped over to the bed and gathered the baby, who had just awoken, into her arms. Then she turned and faced Julia. She was smiling with relief. but her eyes were definitely hostile. With her thin brown face and black dishevelled hair she had a gipsy look about her, something flashing and wild that was barely held under control. She was not going to be an easy sister-in-law, yet Julia sensed that there would be loyal friendship in her if one could arouse it.

"I brought him in here in the night," she explained. "He was crying so badly. Where were you that you didn't hear him?"

Nita's lashes dropped over her eyes. Then she said primly, "Kate put me in that room right at the end of the passage, I was afraid it was too far from Timmy, but usually he never wakes. And I sleep like the dead myself." She looked down at the smiling baby. "Were you crying then, my pet?"

"He's sweet," Julia said warmly.

Nita flashed her a look of unguarded friendliness. Then almost at once the tenseness came back to her face, the hungry-cat look that represented something more than physical hunger.

"He is rather nice. He's all I have." Then she said. "Do you like it here?"

Julia felt the crumpled piece of paper crackling in her pocket. She said gaily, "I love it. Come out on the balcony and look at the view. I stand out here in the mornings just to breathe in this wonderful air. But, of course, you will have been here before and seen it."

"I've never been here before," Nita said. She added as an afterthought, "Harry and I lived in Australia. I'm an Australian. I'm not used to these sort of mountains."

She followed Julia out on to the balcony, and stood clutching Timmy as the fresh morning wind, like cold water, swept over them. The sun was shining and every crevice and scree slope was as clear as if the mountains were not more than half a mile distant.

"They seem to brood," Nita muttered. She looked at Julia leaning on the rail of the balcony. "That doesn't look very safe. I should think half the wood in this house is rotten. Who's that down there?"

Julia looked down and saw Dove Robinson taking a short cut across the lawn on her way home. She must have been over to bathe Paul's ankle. Her hair shone like a burning bush in the sun. She had a slow voluptuous walk, the movements of her body visible beneath the flimsy material of her cotton dress.

"That's Mrs. Robinson, the wife of one of the shepherds. She's a nurse and has been looking after Paul's ankle."

"Has she?" Nita murmured. "She looks decorative."

Dove, thought Julia, could have slipped upstairs with that letter and pushed it under her door before anyone was about. She had come over particularly early. She even doubted if Paul were up yet.

"Kate tells me you have some fabulous clothes," Nita was saying. "I should think they would be wasted up here. But I don't suppose you knew what you were coming to. What on earth are you going to do with the house?"

"Oh, I have thousands of ideas," Julia said airily.

Nita went inside and looked round the room.

"There are some marvellous bits among this old furniture. They could be polished and renovated. That chest of drawers, for instance. It looks like mahogany. These high ceilings give you scope, too. A satin-striped wallpaper would be nice in here and an off-white carpet. I adore white carpets in bedrooms, even if they aren't practical."

Her hungry eyes went on assessing the room, and Julia realised with a sudden shock of surprise that she was talking as if she were planning the renovations for her own home.

"Are you planning to stay here?" she asked politely.

The hostility flashed back into Nita's eyes.

"It was Harry's place as well as Paul's," she said.

Before Julia could absorb the thought of having Nita as a constant companion there was a tap at the door, and Lily came in carrying a morning tea tray.

"Good morning, miss," she murmured demurely, her long eyes moving from Julia to Nita. Her lovely young body was held very erect. She contrived to wear her blue cotton overall like a mannequin. One could imagine her in a filmy negligée reclining gracefully on a divan, Julia thought, and she had the certainty that a similar thought must often come into Lily's head. Especially after Paul's joking about lilies of the field.

"Shall I bring another cup, miss?" she asked.

Nita answered. "No, I'll come downstairs. I must heat Timmy's milk. He's starving."

58

As Lily opened the door to go out the wind swooped in through the open balcony windows, billowing the curtains out and making Julia shiver. It was going to be amusing, she told herself firmly, finding out who was playing those childish tricks. There was nothing to be frightened about. Nothing at all.

She sat down to enjoy her tea. But her enjoyment was short-lived. The tea tasted vilely. What on earth was the matter with it? She sipped it again, then hastily set the cup down and shuddered violently. Someone, she thought in sheer astonishment, was trying to poison her!

For a moment she sat quite still, trying to absorb this shocking suspicion. It couldn't be true! The letters—they proved that she had an enemy—but they were harmless enough. This dreadful tea was different. Perhaps already she was dying. She had only taken a sip, but if the poison were deadly enough——

"What on earth are you doing, darling?" came Paul's exuberant voice from the door. "You look petrified."

Julia turned her head. "Paul!" she whispered. She tried to indicate the cup of tea set on her bedside table. Her hand was trembling uncontrollably.

Paul, walking with his stick, came across to her.

"Good lord, you look sick. What can you see? The only other time I saw a girl look as scared as that was when a spider had run up her arm."

"Paul, don't joke! I may be dying! The tea——"

"What's wrong with it? I know Lily slips at times, but she can't be that bad." Before Julia could stop him he had picked up the cup and taken a mouthful of the hot liquid.

"Paul!" Julia screamed. "Spit it out. Quickly! It's poisoned."

Paul went rapidly out on to the balcony and spat with thoroughness.

"Pah!" he said in disgust. Then surprisingly he began to hoot with laughter. "Darling, if only you could see your face! You look at death's door. It's only a mistake of Lily's. She's put salt in instead of sugar."

Julia licked her lips. Of course, that was all it was. She could taste the salt now. How silly to have got so panicky.

"The careless little devil. I'll speak to her," Paul said. "I'll go down now and get you a fresh cup."

"Was your tea all right?" Julia asked slowly.

"Yes, but I don't take sugar. Neither does Mother. What about Nita, I wonder."

"Nita didn't stay up here for hers," Julia said. Suddenly she said, "Mrs. Robinson did your ankle awfully early this morning."

"She hasn't done it. I'm only just up."

"Then why was she over here? I saw her going home not ten minutes ago."

"Probably come to borrow something," Paul said lightly. "She's always doing that. Anyway, what on earth has Dove got to do with it? Oh, I see. You mean she was talking to Lily and distracting her attention, so that the salt went in instead of the sugar."

"I didn't mean that, either." Julia put her hand in her pocket and felt the creased scrap of paper. Any of the three women could have been in the kitchen and slipped the salt in her teacup. Nita had been up looking for Timmy, Dove had come over early, probably borrowing, and Lily, of course, would have been down making the tea. Lily would know which her tray was, but either of the other two could easily have found out which it was.

It was unimportant, it was trifling, it was just another prank in keeping with the anonymous letters. It was to show her she was not wanted.

"Don't be so upset over a silly mistake," Paul said chidingly.

"But you see it wasn't really a mistake," Julia told him quietly. "Because I don't take sugar in my tea either."

Nevertheless, she wanted nothing more said about the matter, and was distressed when Paul raised the subject after breakfast. Davey had just carried Georgina down, and settled her in her chair, and Paul's words were accompanied by the small snuffling from the white-rabbit bundle in the big armchair.

"Oh, Lily," he said to that young woman who was just leaving the room after giving Georgina her cup of hot chocolate, "did you remember that Miss Paget doesn't take sugar in her tea?"

Lily's eyes gave their slight flicker. She didn't look directly at anybody, her eyes always had a sidelong look.

"Yes, sir. I think so. Didn't I?"

"All too well," said Paul who had obviously decided that the episode was no longer a joke. "You substituted salt, which doesn't make a cup of tea exactly a refreshing beverage."

Lily's hand went to her mouth.

"But I'm sure"—she hesitated—"I'm sure I didn't do that. I mean, the salt box wouldn't be near the sugar basin. Anyway, I think I remembered about no sugar. I'm sure I didn't do it."

"What an extraordinary thing!" exclaimed Kate, her little ripe mouth open. "It sounds like a college-boy joke."

Nita gave the smallest giggle. Her look of tension had increased, as if she were full of secret excitement.

"Has someone got a down on you, Julia? Perhaps it was Dove Robinson. Do you remember, we saw her going home?"

"Yes, what was she over here for?" Paul asked.

"To borrow some milk, sir," Lily answered. "But she was only in the kitchen a minute. Anyway, what could she possibly have wanted to do a thing like that for?"

"I wish you'd say no more about it," said Julia lightly. "It doesn't matter in the least. If someone finds it amusing, that's all right. It didn't kill me, as I was afraid it was going to." She laughed, and all at once she was aware that Davey was still in the room watching her with his dark enigmatic eyes. What does he know about it? she wondered suddenly.

Paul banged his fist on the table. "Well, I won't have it. If it was a mistake, well and good. But I won't have that sort of joke played in this house."

He was directing that speech at somebody, Julia divined. Before she could decide who it was a surprising thing happened. The little bundle in the big chair spoke.

"It would be Harry," said Georgina in her piping voice. "I heard him talking last night. He kept me awake. He always loved practical jokes. Didn't he, Kate? Ah yes, there's no doubt it would be Harry."

For a moment there was complete silence in the room. Then Nita made a sound halfway between a gasp and a cry. It ended in a laugh, and laughing in that high cracked way she ran out of the room.

# EIGHT

NITA was disenchanted. That was the vague thing about her that Julia had tried to identify. Now it came to her with certainty. That was the reason for her dry forced composure, her sad mouth, the way her black eyes surveyed everyone with cynical amusement. Something had happened to her, but it wasn't, Julia was sure, grief for the death of a young husband. Grief would have left her soft, tragic-eyed. She was neither of those things. Her thin body was full of some tense emotion that certainly wasn't grief. Even her hysterical laughter now, as she rushed from the room, was from a distress unrelated to grief.

It could have been caused, Julia thought slowly, by anger or frustration. And if that were truly so it meant that Harry was alive. And not far away.

But if Harry were really alive, why should he want to play stupid malicious jokes on her?

Davey had begun a conversation with Paul about bringing the sheep down from the high country for lambing. Kate was pouring another cup of coffee, slopping it into the saucer as if her hand were shaking. Lily was clattering dishes in the kitchen. Nita had disappeared, but if Harry were mysteriously in the house no doubt she had gone to him. This was the time to look.

Unobtrusively Julia slipped from the room. She knew all the rooms on the ground floor, the kitchen, the library, the big front room where Georgina sat all day, the dining room where they had just finished breakfast, and two or three small rooms at the back that were used for lumber rooms. But upstairs she had not seen all the rooms. She particularly wanted to find the room in which Nita had slept last night. She wanted to know why Nita would not have heard her own baby crying.

There was Georgina's cluttered stuffy room immediately opposite the head of the stairs, then Kate's, and beyond that Paul's. On the other side of the passage was the large guest room that Julia had, then the tiny dressing room in which Timmy had been put. Next to that was the bathroom, and then two rooms that had previously been unoccupied. One of these would be Nita's. Julia tapped on the door of the first. When there was no answer she cautiously opened the door and found another lumber room, clearly uninhabited for the bed was buried beneath a pile of old boxes and baggage. She went out and tapped on the slightly ajar door of the second. Again there was no answer. She went in and saw the double bed, unmade, and blankets flung back carelessly.

Nita's bags were on the floor and her cosmetics on the dressing-table. There was no doubt that it was Nita's room. The only curious thing was that there were two pillows side by side in the bed, and each bore the round indentation of a head.

So that, Julia reflected, was why Nita had not heard Timmy crying. At that instant she had that thought there was a sound behind her. She turned swiftly and saw Nita watching her with narrowed sardonic eyes.

"Something you're looking for?" she asked.

Julia threw back her head. No narrow-eyed gipsy like Nita was going to frighten her.

"Not something," she replied coolly. "Someone." She looked deliberately at the dented pillows. "Where's Harry?" she asked. "Why does everyone tell me he's dead when obviously he is here?"

"Who tells you?" Nita asked swiftly.

Who had told her? Only Georgina, and she was in her dotage. Yet it seemed that in a silent subtle way everyone had told her.

"You surely don't take any notice of a crazy old woman," Nita said. "And if you think I shared my bed you're wrong. I'm a restless sleeper. I fling myself all over the place."

"Then why didn't you hear Timmy crying? You said you slept soundly."

"When I go to sleep, I do. Besides there are two rooms between us, and a wind howling in those god-awful trees outside. Would you have heard him? I won't have him put

63

in that room again. He'll come in here with me. It was Kate's fault last night. She was in a bit of a flap at our arrival."

"Why did you come unexpectedly like that?" Julia asked curiously.

Nita went to the dressing-table, took a cigarette from a packet and leisurely lit it.

"Because I have every right to. Even if I'm only a daughter-in-law, Timmy belongs here."

"Of course," Julia agreed, her voice suddenly gentle. "I understand. You were lonely."

"What do you think?" Nita said furiously. "Left like that, trying to fight my way. Of course I was lonely. Though what I will be here I don't know," she added under her breath.

Julia could see her anger and her despair, but still she could interpret no grief in the girl's defiant face.

"They wish I would go away already," she muttered. "Can't you see? Kate looks at me like an interloper every time she raises those baby eyes of hers."

"Don't be absurd. As far as I'm concerned you're welcome here for as long as you like."

Nita gave her a long look which held that curious mixture of contempt and friendliness.

"And how long do you think you will be here?" she murmured.

Julia laughed. "Until Paul divorces me, I imagine."

"You have competition," said Nita airily. "Perhaps Paul will turn out to be a male Borgia."

Julia thought of the way Paul had kissed her last night, and laughed again, happily. "Are you suggesting it was he who played the trick with the salt?"

"Oh no. He'd be clever enough to give you no warning." Nita suddenly shrugged tiredly. "We're talking nonsense. I don't think I shall burden any of you with my company for long. Now get out while I tidy my room. And don't be dumb."

"Dumb?"

"Like getting it into your head that Harry is here. That's just a piece of imbecile cruelty. If the old lady doesn't stop it I'll throttle her."

Julia thought she understood at last. Nita was too proud to show grief. She preferred to be full of anger and bitterness at the unkind destiny that had robbed her of a young husband. One had to feel deeply sorry for her. She meant to discuss with Paul what could be done for Nita as soon as she got him alone.

But getting him alone seemed to be difficult today. First he was with Davey in the dining room, then he was shut in the library having a long discussion on the telephone. After that again Julia saw him in the garden talking to Nita. He gave her a careless slap across the shoulders, and looked down at her earnestly as if he were reassuring her about something. Julia waited to hear him come in, but when he did Kate waylaid him.

"Is she going to behave?" Julia heard her say in a tense hard voice. It was the voice she had heard outside her bedroom on the night of her arrival, an indication of the unexpectedly fearful uncertain person who dwelt beneath Kate's frivolous light-hearted surface.

"Yes, indeed. I've fixed her," said Paul. Then he added in irritation, "Why do you get so stewed up? Haven't I told you there's no need?"

Julia, on an impulse, went flying down the stairs.

"What's going on here? Is there something I haven't been told?"

Her appearance took them by surprise. She caught on Kate's face a naked look, the anxious frightened person looking out beneath the sophisticated make-up, and on Paul's the disturbing hardness that it had worn last night when she had held up the lighted match to look at him.

In an instant, however, they were themselves again, smiling at her, with Kate saying, "The way you run down those stairs, dear child, you'll break your neck one day. Look at the colour she has, Paul. It's not out of a box, either."

"She's a pretty thing," said Paul lightly.

Julia was impatient. "You're just changing the subject. What were you saying before I came down, something about fixing somebody. Is it about the salt in my tea?"

Paul patted her shoulders. "Perhaps. Forget it, darling. It won't happen again."

Into Julia's mind came vividly the recollection of Paul, a

65

few minutes earlier, patting Nita in a precisely similar way. She drew back rather sharply, then saw his look of hurt surprise and was sorry for her involuntary action.

"Are you cross with us, darling?"

"No, of course not. It was a silly joke, I suppose. But I keep thinking there's something going on under the surface. All this talk of Harry, for instance. I'm going to live here. Haven't I a right to know?"

"The talk of Harry," said Kate sadly, "is only done by poor old Granny. You mustn't listen to her, dear. She's crazy."

"Not all the time," Julia persisted. "We had a perfectly rational talk last evening."

"All the time, I'm afraid," Paul said. "Even when she seems rational."

Kate was dabbing at her eyes with her handkerchief.

"If only what she said were true——"

"Now, Mother," said Paul, "don't get upset. Tell us, Julia, is there anything else that worries you besides Granny's hallucinations and that poor joke about the salt in your tea?"

Julia looked at him wordlessly. She wanted to burst out with all the vague things that troubled her, the way Paul was not the person she remembered, exciting, yes, but not the quiet comfortable person she had known, the way the house and farm were in such a state of careless disrepair, why Nita had arrived so unexpectedly, bringing her restless unhappiness with her, why Kate, who should have been, by her appearance, a light-hearted superficial person, ambitious only for expensive clothes and luxury, had that frightened person living beneath her sophistication, even more vaguely the thought of those two attractive young women, Dove Robinson and Lily in the kitchen pouring cups of tea, her eyes full of guile. And Davey, the intellectual shepherd who knew a great deal more than he was ever going to tell. Most of all the Paul she didn't entirely know, with whom she could make love, but to whom she couldn't talk.

But all she could say flatly was, "The letters."

"Letters?" Paul's thick golden eyebrows lifted.

Julia realised that she had not meant to tell anyone about those childish letters, hoping that whoever wrote them would finally give up her ineffectual persecution. Now the information had slipped out, and Kate was looking at her with a polite interest that scarcely covered her apprehension.

"Anonymous letters," she said, trying to speak lightly. "All of them warning me not to marry you. Are you a Bluebeard or something, darling?"

"When did you get these letters?" Paul asked in a hard clipped voice.

"Oh, they've been following me about ever since I arrived in New Zealand."

"Good heavens! It must be someone who knows my past! But I don't think I'm that bad. Really I don't."

His whimsical sincerity was charming. Why did she not quite believe it? (The lines round Kate's eyes seemed to have deepened, so that she looked an old woman, in spite of her youthful mouth and her air of amused attention.)

"It's someone in this house," Julia said. "One of the letters was slipped under my door this morning."

"How extraordinary!" Kate gasped. "How impertinent! First the salt in your tea, and now this. Really, Paul, we must do something."

"Do you mind if I see these documents?" Paul asked.

"I tore the first two up. This is the one that came this morning." Julia took the crushed scrap of paper from her pocket and smoothed it out. Paul glanced at the crude printing, and suddenly began to laugh in his explosive amused manner, the way he had done when he had tasted the salt in her tea that morning.

"Paul Blaine is no good for you. Don't be a fool," he read aloud. "The thing's elementary." He deepened his voice dramatically and tapped the paper. "This is the hand of a jealous woman."

"Oh, Paul, how nasty!" Kate said faintly.

"Yes, it is nasty," Paul agreed. "All anonymous letters are nasty. But on the other hand it's a little pathetic, and I suppose unintentionally I'm to blame."

Kate was recovering her composure. "Yes, indeed, you must be," she said with asperity. "It's all that ridiculous flirting you do with the girls. Some day one of them was bound to take it seriously. And see how unpleasant it can be."

67

"Then you know who is doing it?" Julia said.

Paul flung out his hands. "I'm afraid I can't be sure just now. But I'll find out. I'll fix it."

Again Julia thought of Nita, and Paul's light remark a few minutes ago that he would fix her. He was certainly full of confidence. She wasn't at all sure that he was going to be able to fix everything. Even a clever and plausible tongue might not manage all those women. It was all so bewildering when one remembered the shy person Paul had been three years ago—before Harry had died. . . .

"I think you're trying to wear your brother's mantle," she said shrewdly.

Kate drew in her breath too quickly.

"That's exactly what he is doing," she said, her voice high-pitched. "Harry was just too adroit in getting out of tangles, but Paul isn't like that, really. Women flatter him, but underneath he's very sincere. I don't need to tell you that, Julia dear. You know how he has treasured the memory of you all this long time."

"I'm beginning to think," said Julia dryly, "that's it's been too long. I should have come years ago."

Paul laughed, and his eyes, looking into hers, were full of warmth and tenderness. Her vague troubled thoughts left her, and now she wanted only to be taken into his arms. Yet some perverse instinct in her resisted that desire. Paul mesmerised her. She mustn't let it become too easy for him.

"I promise you won't get any more of those letters," he said. "I'll find out who is doing it and stop it."

"Yes, for goodness' sake do," said Kate. "It's utterly awful for poor Julia to be treated like this."

"I agree. Now run along, Mother. I want Julia to pack a bag for me. I have to go to Timaru and stay overnight, darling. I have to see about buying sheep, and other things. I'll stop on the way and see Mr. Peters."

"Who is Mr. Peters?" Julia asked.

"The parson, darling. About our wedding. Well, come upstairs quickly. We have to fix the day, don't we?"

The quick unbearable excitement was flowing through Julia again. She wanted to ask Paul whether his ankle was strong enough for him to go on a long trip like that, and why she could not go with him. But the grip of his hand on hers had her in that wordless spell, and she could only follow him meekly, prepared to do whatever was his bidding. It was only vaguely that she noticed the quick uneasiness in Kate's eyes again, as they left her standing in the hall.

It was the first time she had packed a bag for a man. Folding pyjamas, a clean shirt and socks filled her with a possessive pride. It would be fun to choose Paul's shirts and ties for him, if he would let her do so. And he badly needed new hairbrushes, if the ones on his dressing table were all he owned.

"What about a fortnight from today?" Paul said. "Darling, you pack beautifully."

"Our wedding? Yes, please, darling. Don't let's wait any longer. I thing things will be simpler when we are married."

"Simpler?" His eyes mocked her.

"Don't pretend not to understand me. I mean about those letters and things."

"Forget those letters, will you."

"Yes, of course. I never did take them seriously." From somewhere Julia heard Timmy begin to cry, and she at last asked the question that was nagging at her. "Paul, why did Nita come here?"

"Because she's lonely, poor little devil. She's drifted here and there since Harry died. Someone apparently told her I was getting married, and she wanted to meet you and be your friend. That's why she came."

"One couldn't be her friend," Julia said, thinking of Nita's hostile eyes. "She wouldn't allow it."

"Well—don't fight with her. I know she's prickly. She won't be here long. I'm going to find her a place in Timaru."

"Oh," said Julia slowly. So exit the brunette. . . . What about the blonde and the redhead?

Paul put his arms out. "Don't look at me in that highly suspicious way. Come here, blast you! Do you know you give me no peace of mind? You're too entirely beautiful."

## NINE

THE house was dead without Paul. Not that Julia had time to feel lonely, for as soon as he had driven away the electricians arrived to fix the lights, and when they had gone she decided to make plans for the redecorating of the house. She had thought Kate would be a willing adviser, but strangely she seemed to have lost her enthusiasm. She kept saying,

"I have a headache. I get nervous headaches when I'm upset. Often I have to go to bed. Those letters you have been getting upset me. Anyway," she added, "it's going to be your house. You do as you wish." Once she muttered under her breath, "It's too difficult."

"What's too difficult?" Julia asked. "Getting painters and decorators? But Paul would never expect me to live in the house in this state. You have been saying that yourself all the time."

She became aware that Nita was standing in the doorway, and she had the distinct feeling, in that second, that Kate was afraid of Nita. Perhaps Nita had been behaving badly about Julia getting what she, as Harry's wife, would have shared. Poor Kate was torn between the two of them and wanted to be fair. It was only since Nita's arrival that she had shown this reluctance to discuss the renovations, and, indeed, the wedding also.

Or perhaps the knowledge of those anonymous letters had upset her more than she had shown. After all, one didn't like to think that there was a vindictive woman in the house.

To add to all this Georgina kept reiterating in her piping voice, like a bird giving its good-night twitter, "It's so nice to have the boys back. Like old times. I hope they don't fight, Kate. You remember how they always used to be fighting."

Julia looked at Kate. "Did they?" she asked.

Kate sighed. "Harry used to tease Paul. He was such a mischievous boy."

"But isn't it peculiar," Nita said, "how lately Paul has grown so much more like Harry."

Her voice was quite calm and impersonal, yet beneath its quiet tones Julia could sense again the anger and frustration. She either resented the fact that Paul was alive while Harry was dead, or else Paul's resemblance to Harry aroused too much painful emotion in her.

"Don't you think he has changed, Julia?" she insisted.

Julia was aware that Kate was watching her, her baby blue eyes suddenly still, wiped clear of feeling, like a washed slate.

"Yes, I do," she said. "He used to be so much more quiet, and slower." (The Paul she had known in England would not have been giving careless caresses to every attractive girl he met.) "He was sweet," she said reflectively.

Nita's face had an avid look.

"You mean, you don't think he's so sweet now?"

Julia laughed. "In a different way. After all, then we were both very young. Now . . ." she let her voice grow reminiscent remembering the way Paul kissed her.

It was a moment before she realised that Nita's wary black eyes were reading her thoughts very accurately.

"You're just like all the others," she said contemptuously.

"The others?"

"Oh, everyone falls for him. Don't they, Kate?"

Kate said rather helplessly, "It must have been those nurses in hospital who gave him ideas." The heavy eyelids drooped over her eyes. Her face was a doll's, blank and secret. The fearful person who dwelt behind it was kept well out of sight.

"Harry told me a joke last night, one of his naughty ones, the bad boy." The old lady's voice meandered happily on, oblivious of any undercurrents. "He remembers how I used to enjoy a joke. Do you enjoy jokes, Julia? You'll need to, if you marry Harry. I wonder, dear, if you would ask Mrs. Bates to get my wedding dress out and air it, so the moths won't get in it. Mrs. Bates always has to be reminded to do that."

"Granny, Mrs. Bates isn't here any longer," Kate said. "Lily will look after your dress for you."

Georgina's tiny pink face crumpled into scanty tears.

"Oh, I miss Mrs. Bates. Why did you send her away? You were very unkind." She muttered on unhappily for a little while, then she said, quite clearly, "I don't like that Lily. I don't trust her."

Kate sighed. "Now she's going to go over and over that again."

"Julia, are you very much in love with Harry?" Nita clapped her hand to her mouth. "Oh, my God, now I'm catching it from Granny. With Paul, I mean."

"Of course," said Julia serenely.

Nita stood up abruptly. "I don't see how you will be able to stand it," she said and went out of the room.

Kate instantly moved over to sit by Julia. Her eyes, now, were conspiratorial.

"Don't take any notice of Nita. The poor child is just very lonely and unhappy, and I'm afraid Paul reminds her too much of Harry. She mustn't stay here. It's too distressing for her. Don't let her upset you, my dear."

Kate patted Julia's hand. A gust of her perfume filled Julia's nostrils, and suddenly Julia had a stifling feeling of revulsion. She was aware, all at once, that she didn't like Kate. She should have been just a kind-hearted shallow person, but she was hiding some other characteristic beneath her friendly exterior, and that was not pleasant. Perhaps, secretly, she did not want Paul to marry Julia. Perhaps she was the author of the anonymous letters!

It was time someone talked in plain language.

"Is it because of Nita that you don't want me to start altering the house?"

Kate's heavy eyelids—they were like the thick texture of a lily petal—dropped again.

"I try to be tactful, dear. It really is painful for Nita. And she isn't going to stay. Paul is arranging something for her while he is in Timaru. Couldn't you just wait a day or two?"

"Do you think it's Nita who has been writing those letters?"

"Oh no, no! I'm sure it isn't. After all, why should she?

72

She doesn't care about Paul. It was poor Harry whom she loved so much. Oh, no, not Nita."

"Then who?"

Kate flung up her hands agitatedly. "How do I know? Paul said he would stop it, didn't he? Try not to worry about it, dear."

"I know Paul said he would stop them," Julia said calmly. "But I want to know who has been writing them. And I intend to find out."

"Harry's the one who likes jokes," came the thin high voice from among the shawls in the big chair. "Oh, he's a bad boy, that one."

It wasn't too difficult to think of an excuse to go across the field to the cottage where Dove Robinson and her husband lived.

It was a small wooden cottage standing bleakly on a hillside among an outcrop of boulders. If there had ever been an attempt at a garden there was no sign of it now, and only the prickly spider-grey matagouri climbed over the recumbent boulders. There was no sun, and the wind from the cloud-shrouded mountains was strong. Julia felt herself blown along the path to the front door which was slightly ajar.

There was the sound of voices somewhere down at the end of the passage, a man's raised angrily, and a woman's, also pitched to a heightened emotion.

"Haven't I told you not to go running over to the big house so often? But you never listen to me! Oh no, I'm your husband but that don't matter a damn!"

"I tell you I have to go over there to do Mr. Blaine's ankle."

"If you ask me, he sprained his ankle on purpose. Likes to make you a Mary Magdalene, doesn't he? Well, it's a part that suits you both, him so high and mighty, you ready to fall like a ripe plum. It's that red hair of yours, you can't trust it."

"You knew I had red hair when you married me."

"Yes. More fool me. Tell me, what are you going to do when your precious Paul gets married? His wife ain't going

73

to want you running up there all the time to stroke his head if he gets a headache."

Dove made some inaudible answer. Her husband said finally,

"It'd do him a power of good if he got busy and did a bit around the farm. Expects me and Davey to do the whole bloomin' lot, lambing and all. Well, he's the loser if half his lambs die in a storm, and that's as likely to happen as not."

Acutely uncomfortable, Julia made to walk softly away, hoping she would be able to get out of sight before either Dove or her husband appeared. Then suddenly she thought, "Why should I pretend to have heard nothing? Paul is going to be my husband. I'm in this, too."

So she knocked again, much more loudly, and instantly the voices in the back of the house ceased. A minute later the door at the end of the passage opened and Dove appeared. When she saw Julia she hastily smoothed her hair, her hands fluttering over her head to hide the colour that was suddenly a banner in her cheeks.

Julia said airily, "Does one knock at the front door or the back? I just came over to ask if you could sew."

"Sew?" Dove was regaining her composure, the colour dying out of her cheeks and her green eyes glinting inquisitively. Julia suspected that she was not often at a loss. In her way, she had as much careless confidence as Paul.

She stepped back. "Won't you come in? We usually sit in the kitchen. It's the warmest room in the house."

Julia followed her down the narrow passage into the long room at the end that was both kitchen and sitting room, a pleasant place with an open fire and shabby comfortable chairs drawn up to it. It flashed into her mind that Paul might find this room pleasant, too, perhaps when Dove's husband was out on a long ride round the sheep.

The husband had left the room now. As Julia entered she caught a glimpse of him passing the window outside, a sturdy stocky man with a skin burnt red with the wind, and tousled coarse brown hair. Dove must find a considerable contrast between him and Paul—Paul whose ankle she liked to massage gently in her strong white hands. . . .

"Tell me," said Julia abruptly, "how did Paul sprain his ankle? I never asked him."

Again, momentarily, the red flag flew in Dove's cheeks. Then she answered, "He tripped on a rock in the dark. He had been out looking after a sick ewe."

Julia wanted badly to believe her. After all, what more reasonable explanation could there be for a twisted ankle. Those rocks that jutted up in the turf looked highly dangerous. (But this hillside was the only place that Julia had noticed the slate-backed rocks in great numbers. And Dove's husband's remark was still in her ears, "It'd do him a power of good if he got busy and did a bit around the farm.")

"Wasn't it lucky you knew how to treat it," she said smoothly. "Did you nurse for long before you were married?"

"Six years," Dove answered.

"Then you would know, too, how long it takes for scarring in a skin graft to fade."

"You mean one like Mr. Blaine's. Oh, quite a long time."

"More than three months?"

"Oh yes. Mr. Blaine had a very successful one. It's scarcely noticeable now."

"No," said Julia absently. "It was awfully silly of him to worry about what I would think of it." (If Paul's operation had been several months ago, what had he been doing in the meantime?) She smiled in a friendly way, and said, "How long have you been here, in this rather desolate spot? Don't you find it lonely?"

Dove answered unsuspiciously. "We came up three months ago when Mr. Blaine and his mother moved into the big house and sent that awful Bates couple away. Actually," she said, "Tom, that's my husband, doesn't like it here much, but the money's good and there's nothing to spend it on, and we want to get some capital. I persuaded him to come. To tell the truth I think it's the loneliest spot on earth, but I stay here because of trying to save some money."

"Then you were the one who applied for the job?" Julia said.

"You mean, did I interview Mr. Blaine? Yes, I did. Tom would have made a mess of it."

(Oh, Paul, did you hire Lily, too? With her seductive body. Then why bring me across the world like this?)

Julia was almost certain now that Dove, with her red hair and impetuous temper, was the one who had written the anonymous letters. If so, they were harmless enough, for Dove, tied to a dull husband, could not provoke much trouble. The thing was pathetic, really. The most disturbing factor was Paul's weakness for attractive women. But perhaps these low round hills covered with their coarse snow-grass and brooded over by the chill mountains had frightened him with their loneliness, too. Now she was here, she told herself firmly, it would be different.

"What I came for," she went on, "was to see if you could help me make some curtains. I've found some absolutely gorgeous material that's never been taken off its roll. Old Mrs. Blaine must have bought it once and never got round to using it. It would make wonderful curtains for the living room downstairs."

"I could cut them for you," Dove answered. Her voice was not friendly yet, but it was a little less grudging. She was recovering from the embarrassing fact of what Julia might have overheard at the door.

"That would be wonderful," Julia said. "Could you come over this afternoon? I thought I'd try to get them done while Paul is away. Lily might be able to help, too."

But there Dove's eyes flashed with contempt.

"Lily," she said, "I would *hardly* think so, Miss Paget."

Julia was left to read what she would into that remark. Was it Lily's inefficiency Dove despised? Or was she simply jealous of her?

The material Julia had discovered was a heavy cream brocade decorated with fleurs-de-lis. It was rich and orna-mental, and it gave Julia great pleasure to handle it and experiment with ways of hanging it. She tried to concentrate entirely on it, and not allow herself to brood at all on the small, disturbing facets of Paul's character which were gradually being disclosed to her. Supposing she discovered that she had been in love with a person who existed only in her imagination? But that couldn't be so. For she had that very precious letter to prove that Paul was really the man she loved. *You are my sun, moon and stars . . .* he had written.

So she knew that under Paul's careless light-hearted exterior there dwelt that sensitive imaginative person who drew her to him as inexorably as tides to the moon.

Nita said she was useless with a needle. Anyway, she was not even politely interested in Julia's plans, and sat curled up on the couch smoking interminably and watching with that scarcely veiled contempt in her eyes. (Why was she always contemptuous? Julia would not let herself fret about that any more than she would about Paul's flirtatious habits.) Kate bustled about, and seemed on the verge, all the time, of proffering eager advice, but clearly Nita's presence prevented her. Kate did not like being weighed down by grief. She would prefer to turn from it and pretend it did not exist. But Nita's dark tense face constantly reminded her that life was not all the bright frothy thing Kate ardently desired. So she was unhappy and uncomfortable in the presence of her bereaved daughter-in-law. Kate did not face realities, Julia decided.

Dove Robinson proved to be surprisingly clever with a pair of scissors, and Lily, under instructions, moved the step ladder about and made measurements.

It should have been fun, Julia thought wistfully. But there were too many women in the room, and all of them were secretive. It was clear that Lily despised Dove as much as Dove despised Lily, and Nita was sardonically amused about them both. The conversation was limited to the commonplace. The only consolation was that Georgina was upstairs taking her afternoon nap so that one did not have her vague distracting remarks to cope with.

"The house needs more light," Julia said energetically, tugging at the old faded red-velvet curtains that darkened the room to a constant twilight.

"You're wasting your time," Nita observed. "You'll never get light into this house."

Was that remark double-edged, as were most of Nita's? The girl waved her cigarette idly, and said, "All those awful trees."

"Oh," said Julia, inordinately grateful for a simple statement at last. "But I plan to have a lot of them cut down. I intend to speak to Davey about it later."

"Davey? What's it got to do with him?"

Julia was aware of the sharpness of Nita's voice. But before she could ponder over it, her tugging at the old hangings disclosed an enormous grey moth that flopped clumsily into her hair.

Julia promptly tumbled off the chair on which she had been standing and screamed, flapping her hands madly.

Kate rushed to her. "What is it, dear? Did you hurt yourself? Is it a spider?"

"No, it's a moth. Ugh!" Julia was shuddering violently. "I can't bear them. I have a phobia about them." She began to laugh shakily as the moth, dazed and half dead, settled on the window sill and folded its wings shiveringly.

Kate expertly gathered it up and flung it on to the fire.

"You silly child! Is that all it was? I thought you had sprained your ankle, at least. I'm afraid you're going to discover more than moths if you set about cleaning out this house.'

"Yes," Nita said in her thin sardonic voice, "moths will be a mere trifle."

It shouldn't have been so unpleasant as it seemed. But suddenly Julia longed passionately for Paul's gay presence to dispel this peculiar secretive atmosphere. I can't cope, she thought, and in her head she began a letter to Uncle Jonathan.

"Paul has been a naughty boy, letting too many attractive women fall in love with him, and now they are taking out their jealousy on me. I can feel them hating me, even though they never say a word. I am afraid they are going to spoil things. . . ."

Then to herself she added, "I won't let them! No, I won't! I'll show them they can't do this."

But the big gloomy room, covered now in a film of dust from the pulled-down hangings, was suddenly too much for her. She left the work in Dove's capable charge (at least it was easy to see that she respected good material too much to ruin it from mere spite), and throwing on a coat went down to Davey's cottage to ask him about cutting down some of the encroaching trees that shut out the sunlight.

78

There was no one at home. After knocking uselessly Julia turned the handle of the front door and went into the living room. She was sure Davey would not mind her waiting there for him. She would rock gently in the old rocking chair and look at the little dusky Canaletto that she was sure was an original.

Who was Davey? How did someone who owned a valuable picture come to be a shepherd on a lonely hill station? Why did Nita look interested at the sound of his name? Why had she imagined that Nita may have been down at this cottage last night when Timmy was crying? She was almost sure that Nita had not come to Heriot Hills merely to visit relations. Ah, no, that young woman would always have a solid purpose behind her actions.

Julia suddenly thought of the two dented pillows in Nita's bed, and she began to rock violently, disliking the thought in her head so much that she tried to dispel it by movement. The rocking chair slithered a little on the polished floor, and she came up against the half-open drawer of the writing desk.

It was merely the corner of her eye that caught the name Paul written several times on a sheet of paper. She didn't want to look closely. She could not bear to pry. She shouldn't be in this room at all, after all it was Davey's private place while he remained at Heriot Hills. But the name shouted at her.

Paul! Why was the name written several times, and in Paul's handwriting, but a clumsy version of it, as if he had been drunk when he had done it?

Or had Paul written it himself, Julia wondered slowly. Davey Macauley with his self-contained air, his educated voice, his enigmatic eyes that always seemed to be mocking her? Who was he? Paul had met him casually and employed him without references on the rather flimsy and high-flown reason that Davey wanted solitude while he wrote a book. Certainly there was enough paper strewn about to make it look as if he were writing a book.

But why this name written so carefully, a little better each time, the way an intending forger would practise a word?

It was all too much. Those women in the house with their malicious secrets had been enough, but that Davey,

79

whose eyes always looked at her with mocking laughter should also be in some intrigue that she couldn't understand was unbearable. She remembered the way he had thrown his coat round her and she had grown warm, the way he had put his hand reassuringly round her elbow and the tears sprang to her eyes.

At the same moment there was a thin wailing sound, and footsteps at the door. In one swift movement Julia pushed the drawer shut behind her and turned.

Davey stood in the open front door with a new-born lamb under his arm. For a moment it looked as if he were pleased to see her. He smiled in a wholly friendly way. Then his face grew deferential and he said,

"This is a surprise, Miss Paget. Did you want me for something?"

"Yes, I did," Julia said confusedly. "I was thinking all those trees round the house that shut out the light—oh, but the poor little lamb!" she cried, coming back to reality.

Davey set the tiny skeleton-thin creature on the floor and looked up quizzically.

"Think you can save it?"

The lamb tottered on its weak legs and collapsed. Julia went down on her knees and felt for its mouth with her finger.

"Of course we can. Warm some milk quickly. I'll get it to suck."

"This will only be one of many," said Davey.

"Oh, how dreadful! But even one is worth while. Don't stand there. Go and heat some milk!"

Davey went and Julia heard him rattling pans in the kitchen as she let the feeble creature nibble at her fingers. It's those mountains, she was thinking. That's why I hate them. They're the enemies of these small defenceless ones. They pour down the icy winds, and send the snow.

"What happens if there's a snowstorm?" she called to Davey in the kitchen.

"We do what we can," he called back. "The ewes should have been brought down into more sheltered pastures long before this."

"Why weren't they?"

"I'm afraid you must ask Mr. Blaine that. I haven't been here long enough."

"Davey, is it true Paul doesn't like farming?"

"What makes you ask that?"

"Oh, just something Tom Robinson said."

"Perhaps he hasn't settled down to it yet. He's been away a long time."

"But he did once," Julia insisted. "When I knew him in England he was terribly homesick for this place. I remember all one evening—we were supposed to be dancing and having a good time—all Paul could do was talk about Heriot Hills. If he loved it like that, surely he must like farming. Why has he been away so long? Why didn't he come back straight after the war, or at least straight after his operation? Because Dove told me that must have been done quite some time ago."

"Why don't you ask him?" Davey suggested.

Julia could make no reply to that. Already she was sorry for her impulsive questions. There was some peculiar thing about Davey that made her confide in him. It was embarrassing and unnecessary. She fondled the tightly curled greasy wool of the lamb until Davey came in with a bowl which he put on the floor. Then she encouraged the lamb to snuffle and splutter while she held her finger in its mouth in the warm milk.

Presently she said delightedly, "He's sucking quite strongly. He'll be all right. I must get a bottle for him. He'll be mine. Can I have him, Davey?"

She looked up and saw the man's long brown intent face above her. Suddenly that inexplicable warmth swept over her again.

"Who are you?" she said.

Instantly his face closed. He indicated the sprawled lamb. "The badge of my trade," he said lightly.

Julia knew that he would say no more. She knew, too, that she could never ask him about that handwriting in the drawer of the writing desk. Nothing would ever be said about it unless some eventuality . . . For a moment she closed her eyes, desperately hating even the thought. Then she pulled herself together and began to tell him calmly about the trees to be trimmed and cut down. From now on her association with Davey Macauley would be purely on a business footing. Because somehow she was afraid of letting it be anything more.

## TEN

It was that night that the moths were in her room. She turned back the sheet of her bed, and they fluttered drunkenly at her, half a dozen, she didn't know how many of the hateful creatures, bumping into her face, slithering over her arms in a mad flurry of feelers and furry wings.

She was nearly demented. She screamed in an ecstasy of terror until Kate, Nita, and Lily came running. Kate instantly summed up the situation, and began flapping at the moths with the voluminous skirts of her negligée until they had all ceased to flutter.

"Goodness," said Nita in her cool drawl, "you do have a thing about moths, don't you." She picked up one of the extinguished insects and carelessly flipped it out on to the balcony.

"Someone put them there," Julia gasped.

"Where, dear?" asked Kate agitatedly. "Didn't they come in the window? You should have it shut if you dislike moths so much."

Lily, who was attired only in shapeless cotton pyjamas that yet could not hide the grace of her body, said, "It's a bit early in the year for moths to be about. I expect we shook them out of all those curtains we took down today."

"But why should they come up to Julia's room?" Kate was almost as distressed as Julia. Her eyes seemed to implore Julia not to take the episode too seriously. "I think they have come in from outdoors. It's very mild tonight. Julia dear, I think you need a sip of brandy."

Julia, sitting on the edge of the bed, tried desperately to control her trembling. I mustn't let them see how vulner-

82

able I am, she told herself. It only gives them more weapons. Someone is doing this to upset me while Paul is away. Someone who hates my being here.

"I'll be all right now," she managed to say. "I'm ashamed of myself. I don't know why I dislike moths so much. I'd rather have tarantulas crawling over me." She attempted to laugh. "Well—the battle's over. I'm sorry I disturbed everyone."

"Poor little girl," said Kate, patting Julia's shoulder with her fat white hand. Julia was aware that it trembled slightly. "I shall bring you a hot drink, no matter what you say. Lily, run downstairs and put the kettle on."

Lily obeyed, and Nita, also, turned to go. But in her acid manner she could not resist a parting remark.

"Wherever the moths came from, you know who Granny will blame." Her brilliant black eyes rested on Julia, her mouth twitched slightly in that tense overstrung way. "Don't you?" she said.

"Now don't take any notice of her either," said Kate. "I don't know why so many absurd things are said in this house. It's like"—her lips quivered with their easy emotion—"it's like reviling the dead."

When the hot milk, in which Kate had insisted on putting a spoonful of brandy, came Julia would not drink it. She was grateful that Kate who had a nervous headache from the disturbance and was anxious to get to bed, at last left her alone so that she could leave the glass untouched. Because who knew what might be in it? Perhaps now she was being unduly suspicious. But anyone who had observed that afternoon the terrified disgust moths aroused in her and could deliberately play this horrible trick on her was quite capable of putting something unpleasant in her drink.

She could not sleep that night. She longed passionately for Paul to be home again, so that at least she might know he was in the house and not be left entirely to the mercy of some unknown woman. She lay listening to the wind in the trees, and occasionally, as she remembered the fluttering moths, a ripple of revulsion went over her body. Finally she was glad she could not sleep, for she intended to be up at daylight the next morning and listening. The mo-

ment she heard the faintest sound in the passage she
would whip her door open and see who prowled by. Thus
she would unmask her persecutor.

But after all she slept. The sun was shining when she
awoke, and the slip of paper, folded cheekily in the shape
of a paper hat was under her door.

Slowly she got out of bed and went to pick it up and
read its malicious message.

*How can you trust Paul Blaine's honeyed tongue? You
are like a moth caught in a flame.*

She had scarcely finished reading the note before there
was a sound in the passage, a shuffling scraping noise just
at her door. Julia flung the door open and almost knocked
over Georgina who was making her slow painful way towards the bathroom. With her little hunched back she was
bent almost double, her fine white hair fluffed over her
face so that she might have been a rabbit hopping on all
fours.

"Can I help you, Granny?" she asked.

"No, my dear. I can manage if I take my time." The old
lady turned her mild, kind eyes on Julia. "Is that naughty
boy Harry leaving letters under your door now? I thought
I saw him a few minutes ago."

Julia was suddenly clutching the old lady's frail shoulders.

"Who did you see, Granny? Tell me."

"Why, I think it was Harry, dear. But I don't see very
well, you know. And he wouldn't stop when I called. But
it may have been a woman. I couldn't say. It's only that if
there's mischief you can be sure Harry is the culprit."

Paul arrived home in the middle of the afternoon. He
drove up to the front door with a flourish, honking his
horn madly, then came inside with his arms full of parcels.

There had been so much Julia had wanted to ask him,
suspicious things all of them, that she wanted him to dis-
miss, with frank, simple answers. But when he was there
before her she could not say one word. His vitality filled
the house and gloom and tension had vanished. Julia wanted
to laugh for happiness. Darling Paul! She was so glad to see
him again. He brought with him gaiety and reassurance

84

and safety. Safety? Her mind slurred over that query. She let Paul take her in his arms and kiss her warmly, the slight tickling of his golden moustache titillating that secret laughter within her.

"Hey, what's wrong with you?" he asked. "You got a joke?"

"A nice one," Julia said, rubbing her fingers over the soft golden hairs of his upper lip.

"If it's me, I agree with you. I'm a poor joke for any girl. Look, I bought a new car for Nita, and this is all I have for you."

He held up a small square parcel tantalisingly out of her reach.

"Oh, Paul! How exciting! What is it?"

"Don't you want to know about Nita's car first?"

"Car?" That was Nita's voice from the doorway, a dry sceptical voice on an upward inflection.

Julia looked up and saw her standing there, a slight, vivid figure in a red sweater, her dark eyes glinting. It occurred to her vaguely that since Nita had arrived the other night she was never out of earshot. On a provocation remark she appeared like a genii. It could be, of course, that she listened at doors.

"Yes, I bought you a car," said Paul casually. "It's in Timaru. You can take delivery whenever you please. I've also rented a flat in Timaru for you and Timmy. It's quite large and it overlooks the bay. I think you will like it."

Nita took a step down the stairs.

"But why all this munificence?" Her voice was wary and suspicious, and Julia wanted to shout at her not to spoil Paul's marvellous generosity by her inevitable suspicion.

"You deserve it," Paul said. "After all——" He stopped, but his sympathetic voice implied the rest. Harry was dead, while Paul was happily alive; Paul was marrying the girl he loved, while Nita was a lonely widow. Yes, it was fair that Paul should buy Nita things and try to comfort her. But why did she look so ungrateful?

"Well," said Nita softly, "I didn't know there was so much money in the family." Her swift gaze round the shabby hall was eloquent. Then she seemed to remember her manners at last, and she added eagerly, "What sort of a car is it? I'm longing to see it. Couldn't I have it out here?"

"I hardly thought it was worth while bringing it out," Paul answered. "I didn't think you would be wanting to stay."

Did some secret message pass between them? Julia couldn't be sure, but for some reason Nita suddenly became acquiescent.

"You're quite right. I'm not crazy about the country. Actually, I loathe it. Thank you very much, Paul. I shall go and take possession of my new home in Timaru."

Paul smiled in his warm friendly manner.

"We'll have a house-warming for you. After the wedding."

"Oh yes," Nita cried, in her tense excited manner. "Do let's do that. Promise!"

Then Kate appeared, delighted to see Paul back, and Paul groped among the packages which he had dropped carelessly on the floor when he had kissed Julia.

"Here you are, Mother," he said, handing her a long flat box. "That's your share."

"My share, darling?" Kate enquired, her blue eyes irrepressibly eager at the prospect of an unexpected gift.

"For the wedding," said Paul. "Well, open it."

Kate needed no second admonition. She tore off the wrappings, lifted the lid of the box, and disclosed a blue fox fur.

"Oh-oh!" she cooed. "Paul, my pet! How you spoil me! This is beautiful. I adore furs. But, darling, the expense!"

"Forget it," said Paul lavishly. "I've even bought Davey a thousand sheep. Where are the girls?"

"The girls?"

"Lily and Dove. You don't suppose I could forget them?"

Nita suddenly burst into excited laughter. "Paul, you've come into money. I know it!"

"Don't be silly," said Kate with sudden uneasiness in her voice. "Where would Paul come into money? He's merely spending his hard-earned savings. I think he's being extremely reckless."

Paul wagged his finger.

"Now, Mother! I'll take that fur back."

Kate clutched at it, her eyes full of desire.

Paul laughed. "Then don't be a spoil-sport. You wear that thing before the moths get into it."

His glance went round the three women, aware of the sudden silence. "What's wrong?"

"Oh, nothing," siad Kate quickly. "Nothing at all. It's just that Julia has a thing about moths. They worried her last night."

"At this time of the year?" Paul questioned.

"Oh, we'd been pulling down hangings. We disturbed them. Great flopping things. Paul, did you arrange about the wedding?"

It seemed to Julia that Kate had changed the subject too quickly. She seemed to get unaccountably nervous when Paul was about.

Paul slipped his arm round Julia's waist.

"I did, indeed. Wednesday week, as ever is."

There was a short silence. Then Nita said, "I must tell Dove and Lily. They'll be enchanted." Her eyelids drooped with their deliberate secretiveness. "About their presents, I mean."

Julia's gift from Paul was a necklet of seed pearls. "To wear round that delicious little neck on your wedding day," he said. And suddenly, for no reason at all, Julia was seeing the insolent writing on the scrap of paper—*How can you trust Paul Blaine's honeyed tongue?*

She wouldn't let herself start wondering how Paul could suddenly have so much money to spend, when the house and farm were in such a sad condition of disrepair and neglect. She lovingly clasped the pearls round her neck and said, "I must go and see what they look like. They're beautiful, Paul."

In her room an impulse took her to open the wardrobe and look into its cavernous depths at her wedding dress, shining like a white flower. The pearls, Paul's lovely gift, would be perfect with it. Suddenly she wanted to see how they did look. She stripped off her jumper and skirt and began to array herself in the wedding dress.

She hadn't had it on since showing it to Uncle Jonathan before leaving France. She had dressed up in it so that he should get a glimpse of the bride whom he, in his peculiar, vicarious way, was substituting for the girl he had never married. She remembered the way he had looked as he saw her, his thin old face full of a wry pleasure.

"You have made me very happy," he had said. "I have had a lonely life, I don't mind telling you, but your ,and Paul's marriage at the end of it is very satisfying to me. Do you understand that?"

"Because Paul is your Georgina's grandson?" Julia asked.

"I'm a sentimental old man in my dotage. But it's pleasant to end one's life with a little flourish."

Julia turned slowly in front of the mirror. The pearls lay softly round the hollow of her throat. She imagined walking slowly towards Paul down the aisle, and him turning to look at her with his warm, admiring gaze, but her eyes remained unlighted. She looked remote and somehow unreal. A snow maiden, she thought, and involuntarily she looked towards the high peaks that shone chilly and austere beyond the trees. She began to shiver slightly. Why, she wondered, did she always feel cold in Uncle Jonathan's beautiful dress?

There was a call from downstairs. "Julia! Julia dear, come quickly!" It was Kate in her excited child's voice, and Julia, without thinking, went to the head of the stairs.

She didn't know that both Dove and Lily were going to be down there looking up at her. Nor that Paul was still there and seeing the dress she hadn't meant him to see until her wedding day. The hall seemed to be full of faces, and suddenly there was the last one of all, Davey's, still and without expression, as he paused at the door on his way in.

"Oh, my goodness, it's *beautiful!*" That was Kate, spontaneously speaking her feelings. "How sweet of you, dear, to dress up for us."

"I didn't dress up for you," Julia said in a small cold voice. Now she was beginning to shiver violently, for no reason at all. The upturned faces of the four women were too much for her, because one of them, Nita with her hungry eyes, Dove quick-tempered and difficult, Lily silent and sly, was deeply and vindictively jealous.

She gathered up her skirts. "You aren't supposed to be seeing me. But Kate called——"

"It was to tell you to come and see Dove's and Lily's

presents, dear. But you have put everything in the shade."

"My, my!" said Paul softly. "Why haven't I seen that before?"

"Don't be silly, Paul," said his mother. "The bridegroom isn't supposed to see the bride until the wedding day. Is it bad luck? Oh no, it can't be. Just a superstition or something."

"I'm awfully superstitious about weddings," said Dove in her high clear voice.

Lily giggled suddenly, and turned away, concealing her face.

It remained for Nita to change the subject.

"Give me a cigarette," she said to Paul. She almost snatched the packet from him in her tense nervous way, but when she had lighted the cigarette there seemed to be amusement and that undercurrent of excitement in her voice. "Paul, I've changed my mind. I think I'll have the car sent up here. I'd like to stay until after the wedding." Her brilliant black eyes were raised to Julia at the top of the stairs. "It's going to be so exciting!" she murmured.

Davey, who had been at the door a moment ago, had vanished before Julia turned to go.

That evening the dark shreds of clouds that had drifted about the mountain peaks all day moved across the sky, the wind cried on a high eerie note, and a few flakes of snow began to fall.

There was a large fire lit in the big front room downstairs. The new curtains, with their rich texture, were drawn across the windows and the room was full of cosiness. Paul sat on the couch with his foot up, because too much movement had made his ankle swell again and Dove had been angry with him. At least Julia imagined it was anger with a refractory patient that had brought that sharp note to her voice as she had scolded Paul before dinner for his carelessness. It had made Lily giggle again, and Paul had exclaimed in his amused, tolerant way, "You woman make my life too complicated."

Nita was at the piano singing softly in a husky contralto. Kate had been in the winged chair with her novel and a box of chocolates until a few minutes ago when she had had to go upstairs to answer Georgina's impatiently rapping stick. Julia was curled up on the hearthrug as close to the fire as she could get, because that queer shivery cold seemed to be still in her bones. All she could think of was the lovely Lanvin dress dropped in a heap on the floor in her bedroom and the goose-flesh on her arms. Nita sang charmingly, but somehow her song seemed to be part of the cold, a dirge that said, "You'll never wear that lovely dress, because Paul is faithless . . . faithless . . . faithless. . . ."

Paul's fingers caressed her cheek.

"What are you thinking of, love?"

"I'm listening to Nita."

"Darling, do you know how absolutely beautiful you looked this afternoon."

"You shouldn't have seen me," Julia said sadly.

"Why should everyone else be allowed to see you, and not me?" He reached over to rest his lips on the nape of her neck. "Darling, I'm utterly crazy about you."

Julia plucked at the wool of the hearthrug.

"I had another letter this morning."

His voice came quickly.

"I'm sorry, darling. They'll stop now. I know."

"Is that why you bought all those expensive presents?"

Nita sang in her husky hopeless voice, *Goodbye summer, goodbye, goodbye. . . .*

"No, it isn't. Why are you shivering?"

"I don't know. That song—I suddenly thought of grave-yards. . . ."

Paul began to give his hearty explosive laugh. Nita's song stopped in the middle of a bar. Her fingers crashed on the keys.

"What are you two talking about?"

"Can't you sing something more cheerful?" Paul asked. "You're making Julia morbid."

"I feel morbid myself," Nita said simply. She came over to stand by the fire. She was so thin that her figure was a shadow. "It's this damned snow beginning," she said.

"Well, I'm not morbid," Paul said. "I'm exceedingly cheerful because my ankle won't allow me to go round the sheep. Old Davey has the job himself."

Julia turned.

"How long has Davey been gone?"

"Since this afternoon. He came in to tell me he thought it was going to snow."

Julia sprang up.

"Then I must go down and feed the lamb."

"What lamb, darling?"

"The stray that Davey brought in last night. It was nearly dead then but we brought it round. It would be a shame to let it die now."

Paul flung out his hands.

"Darling, you'll soon learn not to fret about every stray lamb."

Perhaps she would, too, but this lamb was special. It represented her very first experience in saving a life. If nothing else, there was something about Davey's cottage that always brought her back to sanity. Even without Davey there it had a reassuring effect, and now she wanted to escape from the peculiarly morbid mood that Nita's singing had produced in her. She flung a coat over her shoulders, and groped her way through the thinly falling snow to the cottage.

Davey was not there. The lamb in the kitchen called feebly at the sound of her entrance. She switched on lights and found the little creature in its box snuffling hungrily. The cottage was very cold. Julia put on milk to heat for the lamb, then built up a fire of slow-burning coal in the living room. When she had fed the lamb and it had settled down contentedly she stayed by the fire, watching the reflections of the flames on the walls, listening to the wind and wondering when Davey would come home. She felt as safe and contented as the warmed and fed lamb. When at last she got up to go it was only because her eyelids were drooping with sleep, and it would hardly do for Davey to find her asleep on his hearth.

She put a screen in front of the banked fire and went out. The snow had stopped and there was a little thin moonlight. The path, speckled with snow, showed quite clearly, and she had no trouble in finding her way beneath the dripping trees to the big house.

There were no lights showing. She had a momentary feeling of surprise that Paul had not waited up for her, then she was obscurely grateful that he had not. She wanted only to creep upstairs undisturbed and get into bed.

She opened and closed the frong door softly, groping her way to the front of the stairs without putting on a light. It was as she felt for the banisters that she heard a faint scuffling sound from the direction of the passage that led to the kitchen. Then, perfectly clear, came the low deep voice.

"Now are you going to behave yourself?"

There was a faint, unidentifiable chuckle. Then, "Yes, Harry darling," came on a deep sighing breath.

"Who's there?" Julia asked sharply. She went quickly forward in the darkness, and as she reached the kitchen door she felt for the light switch.

A hand closed over her wrist. In the same instant another one went firmly over her mouth. Before she could struggle she was pushed firmly back into the passage and the door closed behind her. She heard the click of the lock.

She raised her clenched hands to beat on the door. Then she dropped them to her sides hopelessly. What was the use? No one would answer her outcry. If she ran upstairs screaming for help because Harry, who was not dead at all, was making love to somebody in the kitchen they would all look at her in astonishment. And by the time she had routed them from their beds, Harry and the woman with him (who was it—Dove? Lily? Nita?) would have vanished.

In any case she felt as if nothing of this were really happening. She was in the dream that had held her in thrall all the time she was in this big derelict house.

Perhaps she hadn't heard those voices. Perhaps no one had seized her wrist.

She began to stumble bewilderedly to the stairs.

There was a faint chink of light across the landing upstairs.

"Julia, is that you?" came Kate's voice.

"Yes, Kate."

"How late you are, dear. Paul said something about going to look for you. Are you all right?"

Julia went to Kate's door and looked in.

"Yes, I'm all right. Harry's in the kitchen. I suppose you know."

Kate, in a fluffy pink bedjacket that made her look like an oversized doll, sat bolt upright, her hand to her mouth.

"Harry! What *are* you talking about?"

"I wish I knew," Julia said wearily. "But he's there. I heard someone call him by name. I suppose he's the person who has been doing those peculiar things, the moths and so on. But why?"

"My dear child!" Kate began to climb out of bed and grope for her slippers. "You're crazy. I must get Paul."

There was a movement behind Julia, and there was Paul in a dressing-gown, his hair tousled, his cheeks flushed as if with sleep.

"What's the matter, darling? Why does Mother say you're crazy?"

"Harry's in the kitchen," Julia said flatly. "But it's no use your going down. He'll be gone by now. Only I wish someone would just tell me why there is all this mystery about him."

Paul went leaping down the stairs two at a time. He switched on the light in the hall and disappeared in the direction of the kitchen. Julia followed him slowly. She fancied she heard a splutter of laughter. But she must have imagined it, because when she reached the kitchen Paul was in it alone. The fire was out in the stove, and the room had a completely deserted look.

"There's no one here," he said.

"There was a moment ago," she insisted stubbornly.

"Is Davey at the cottage yet?"

"No."

"But he must be back by now. He probably came in here to speak to Lily. She makes him a hot drink when he's round the sheep late."

Julia's eyes mutely swept the empty table and bench.

"Well, perhaps he didn't have a drink tonight," Paul said impatiently. "But that's no doubt who it would be. Want me to go down to the cottage?"

"No," said Julia, shaking her head. "I'll ask Lily in the morning." (Now are you going to behave yourself? Yes, Davey darling. . . ." Was that the way it had been? Had she imagined the name Harry because she, like Georgina, was getting an obsession about him?)

"Yes, do that," said Paul. "Though mind you, the minx will only tell you what she pleases. She's a deep one."

Julia was too weary even to question that remark. She couldn't imagine why the thought that it had been Davey with Lily in the kitchen was so distasteful to her. Perhaps because she had been waiting fruitlessly by that fire she had lit for him.

"I'll go to bed," she said.

"Yes, darling. That's the best thing. I waited for you until I damn near fell asleep myself. I thought you must have been talking to Davey. What were you doing?"

"Nothing," said Julia vaguely.

Paul's eyes searched her face quizzically. Then he put his soft full lips against her cheek.

"You're dead on your feet. My little stupid!"

His caress roused no feeling at all in her.

Kate, her fingers pressed to her temples, was waiting shivering at the head of the stairs.

"Well?" she said.

"Go back to bed, Mother," said Paul. "There's no one there."

"Oh, I'm so glad." Kate's eyes on Julia were reproachful. Perhaps she thought that what with anonymous letters, moths, and ghosts in the kitchen, Julia was becoming too fanciful for comfort. Yet Julia, for all her weariness, had the feeling that Kate was using reproach to cover her too-apparent fear. If she were not so tired, she thought, she would get the clue to this.

But she could only smile faintly in contrition for her behaviour and go silently to her room.

As she opened the door the curtains from the long windows billowed out and a flurry of half-melted snow came into the room. The air was icy.

How had she come to leave the windows open? Julia ran to close them, shutting out the cold wind and the sound of the swaying trees. Then she stood quite still. For she was absolutely certain that she had closed and bolted the windows securely before dinner that night.

In the morning it had stopped snowing, but the sky was

just above the treetops, heavy and grey. Julia, waking late and reluctantly, found Lily at her bedside with her morning tray.

"Good morning, miss," Lily said. "It's a horrid day. Mrs. Blaine said you ought to have a morning in bed. And there was this note under your door."

She handed the folded slip of paper to Julia and went briskly to the door.

Julia's fingers trembled so that she could scarcely unfold the scrap of paper. The message was simple and juvenile, and vindictive, as usual.

*Don't you know that you will never wear that beautiful dress to marry Paul Blaine.*

## ELEVEN

THE bus, on its way to Mt. Cook, left the mail at midday. There were letters from Uncle Jonathan at last, one for Julia and one for Paul. Tom Robinson, dressed in oilskins, had brought the bundle of mail from the gate and handed it to Julia.

"Weather's getting worse," he said. "Davey and I were out most of the night, but we're going to lose a lot of lambs."

"Most of the night?" Julia repeated sharply. That meant, then, that it was unlikely Davey had been in the kitchen. She had never believed that he had.

Tom Robinson nodded. "It was tough on Davey. He's not used to it."

Julia absently rifling through the letters in her hand, suddenly lost the gist of his remarks entirely. For she found herself looking at a name on an envelope. "Mr. Harry Blaine, Heriot Hills. . . ."

Tom had shuffled off in his heavy boots and oilskins before she realised he had gone. Paul came behind her and quietly took the bundle of mail from her.

"Some for me?" he asked.

"Paul! There's one for Harry."

Paul quickly studied the typewritten address.

"I'll fix that. Don't let Mother see it. It upsets her."

"But what is it?"

"It will be some overdue subscription or something. This sort of thing happens after a man dies. Didn't you know? Ah, this looks like your Uncle Jonathan's handwriting."

"Yes, it is. I have a letter from him, too. Paul, what are you hiding from me?"

He laid a hand on each of her shoulders. He was smiling, and his eyes were kind, but beneath their kindness was an implacable look.

"Darling, once and for all I am the only man in this house. There is no mystery. Nothing is being hidden from you. I and I alone own this beautiful harem. Do you understand that? Granny is old and suffers from delusions, but you don't. You have no excuse at all for this sort of thing. So drop the subject, will you?"

It was a command. Julia levelly returned his gaze, and had no intention whatever of obeying.

"Then why did I get another letter this morning?"

Paul's face darkened. "I haven't had time to go into that yet, but I promise you whoever is doing it will leave. Even if it's our valuable Lily. Can you cook, darling? It might be necessary for a few days."

"Supposing it's Dove," Julia said.

"Dove also will go. I tell you I'll stand no nonsense over anything concerning you. Now, does that please you?"

Julia knitted her brows.

"Paul, you're so different. Once you were so shy, even with me. Do you remember that you only kissed me once? And now I find you with your harem, as you call it, and myself bitterly hated. It's a little hard to adjust oneself."

That, of course, brought her into his hard embrace.

"You don't like me," he said, his breath on her cheek, his voice full of that confidence that was almost displeasing.

But her body melted and her lips murmured of their own accord.

"You get your own way too easily. You haven't been fair

to those poor girls." She tugged his nose gently. "You have to behave."

"I'll behave," he promised, his quick charming smile smoothing that faint strangeness out of his face. "Now let's see what your excellent guardian has to say."

A few moments later Paul gave his loud explosive hoot of laughter. Julia was beginning to recognise that particular laugh. He gave it when he was upset or embarrassed or surprised.

"What is it?" she asked.

"Nothing. The old boy's full of advice, that's all." There was a high flush in his cheeks. Suddenly he crumpled the letter in his hand and flung it into the fire.

"Paul!"

He turned, his eyes sparkling with anger.

"Sorry, darling. But your worthy uncle doesn't seem to trust me awfully. I don't altogether appreciate his attitude."

"But, Paul, what did he say? And that's nonsense about his not trusting you. After all, he was the one who urged me to come out to New Zealand."

"So you needed urging?"

"Paul!" She laid her hand on his arm. "You know I didn't. Don't be so contrary. And whatever Uncle Jonathan said, remember he's an old man with impossibly high ideals. Why, he still thinks of his poor old Georgina as a young and beautiful girl. You'd have to be a saint to come up to his standards."

"And I'm no saint," said Paul violently.

His angry excitement worried her. What *had* Uncle Jonathan in his fumbling earnest way said? She had to try to soothe him.

"And how do you think I'd like being married to a saint?" She was almost going to say she preferred the complexities of several attractive women about the house. But that would make Paul's mood worse. "Don't worry about it, darling. I wish you hadn't burnt that letter. I'd like to know what the silly old man did say."

Paul's eyes glinted with a sudden almost uncontrollable excitement.

"Would you, then," he muttered. "I'm afraid you never will."

"Paul it's your vanity that's been hurt."

He began to laugh in his sudden, loud, nervous way.
"That's what it is," he admitted. "Do you think I won't
make you happy?"

Before she could answer he was bending over her, holding her hurtingly and pressing his lips against hers.

"God, I want you!" he muttered. "And I'm going to have
you. Nothing will stop me."

"Paul darling! Of course you are. What are you talking
about?" She was a woman soothing a refractory child. She
was also ever so faintly frightened.

Uncle Jonathan's letter to her was upsetting only in
one way. The old man said that he had very little time
left to live. He said, "Write to me as soon as possible. I
want to hear all about your new life. Tell me about Paul.
Will he make you a good husband? Be quite sure of that
before you marry him, my dear. I believe that happiness
can be assisted by sensible and practical behaviour, but it
also must have its base on a firm foundation. From what I
knew of Paul when he was in England with us I am sure
that foundation will be there. Nothing will give me a greater
satisfaction than to hear you confirm this belief. And now
—some news of Heriot Hills, and my dear Georgina. Does
she remember me? What does she say? I know she will be
very old. Appearances are nothing to me now. It is the heart
and the spirit that matter. Write soon, my darling child. It
is your future that is my constant concern. . . ."

No, there was nothing there to arouse anger. All Julia
could feel was a great sadness that the man who had
been a father to her, and who had always loved her de-
votedly, would soon no longer exist. She could not imagine
the world without Uncle Jonathan.

She wanted to sit down and answer his letter at once.
But it was too difficult. How could she tell him about
Georgina? "They say she is crazy. She imagines her grandson Harry is in the house, and Harry is dead. She snuffles
like a little animal. She is flesh and blood and no more
at all. . . ." How could she tell Uncle Jonathan that? Julia
sat on the windowsill watching the thickening snowflakes
and pondering sadly on the gradual and inexorable death
of earthly love. One day she and Paul would grow to be

98

like that. She would feel no sensation at all when his lips touched her. How could so vivid a sensation die?

What could she tell Uncle Jonathan? "Paul has grown very vain and he behaves badly with girls, he flatters them and no doubt makes love to them and means nothing. All kinds of complications arise, but still I forgive him and forget the unpleasant happenings, so I must love him in the way you mean. . . ."

She could write none of those things. Could she say, "What did you put in your letter to Paul to make him so angry? You must have offended his vanity. It is the privilege of the old to be frank, but I think, my darling uncle, that you must have overstepped that privilege a little."

The thoughts fluttered through her head like the whirling snowflakes outside. It was the premature darkness and the silence that was making her depressed and lonely. It wasn't because she imagined she had made the sad discovery that one could go on being lonely even with the man one loved.

It was Timmy's waking that roused her from her depression. Once before Timmy's plump little arms round her neck had comforted her. She loved the little boy whom Nita cared for but emotionally seemed to ignore. Perhaps he reminded her too much of his father. She picked him up from his cot and changed him and carried him downstairs to the fire, where Georgina was gently nodding and murmuring to herself.

Georgina's filmy eyes seemed to clear slightly at the sight of Timmy.

"What a beautiful baby, Julia dear. But I didn't know you and Harry had been married so long."

Timmy held out his hands and cooed to the funny little white bundle in the chair. Georgina nodded and smiled.

"So wonderful," she said. "Almost as if Jonathan and I had been married after all."

Julia was on the point of correcting her. Then it didn't seem worth while. For probably one day what the old lady imagined would be true. Or true with the exception that the baby would be Paul's and not Harry's.

The thought filled her with excitement and something almost approaching dread.

Then, as if Paul had been aware of her thoughts, he suddenly came in. He sat down on the hearthrug beside Timmy and began rolling him about until the child screamed with laughter. He looked up at Julia under his thick golden lashes.

"How about us having one of these?"

"Perhaps."

"Quickly. Don't let's waste any time."

She felt the excitement and dread stirring in her.

"Paul, I didn't know you were so crazy about children."

"I would be about ours."

Neither of them had noticed Nita come in. She seemed to swoop over Timmy suddenly like a jealous and angry bird.

"You get your own," she said to Julia. "This one's mine."

Julia had not noticed before that when Nita was excited about something her eyes had a very slight cast. She noticed it now, and it accounted for the illusion that Nita, as she spoke was not looking at Timmy, but at Paul.

"Paul," she said, as Nita went out, "I've never seen a photograph of Harry. Are you very like him?"

"Probably. Why?"

"Sometimes I think Nita is falling in love with you."

He put back his head and gave his derisive hoot of laughter.

"Darling! It's a constant embarrassment to me, but all the girls seem to do that. And *I* love only you."

"Sometimes," she said slowly, "I think you're never serious. Why, you don't even take Heriot Hills seriously. Look at the state you have let it get into. You used not to be like that."

"I've been ill," he said. "I told you that."

"But since then, Paul. You had your operation a long time ago. Didn't you?"

He lifted his eyes and they were wide with that innocent choir-boy look that was so irresistible.

"What makes you think that?"

She touched his face lightly. "This scarring is almost invisible. You must have expected me to know that would take some time."

He dropped his eyelids. "I was still ill," he muttered.

"Oh, Paul!" She was full of contrition. "What was the matter?"

"Oh, a kind of a breakdown. I'd worried too much. My frightful conceit."

She was nearly in tears.

"Paul, you should have told me this."

"I was afraid if I told you you mightn't love me as much," he said simply.

"How utterly ridiculous! You great stupid."

The confidence began to come back to his face.

"I can see that now. For a while there I wanted every girl I met to fall in love with me, just to prove I could make them."

"You should have told me all this sooner," Julia said.

"I suppose I should. It's still hard to talk about it. Will you be a bit understanding in the future, darling?"

"You mean about getting anonymous letters and things? Of course I will. I'll just be sorry for the person who's writing them, poor thing."

She was very happy for the rest of that day. Everything was clear to her now and she could write to Uncle Jonathan at last.

"Will you be careful, please, Uncle dear, not to put anything in your letters to Paul that might hurt him, because he is extremely sensitive. He has had a bad experience with his illness and it has made him so afraid that I might not go on loving him. And I thought he was over-confident! . . ."

Even Paul's fuming that because of his bad ankle he was still unable to get out and help Davey and Tom Robinson with the ewes and newly born lambs made her happy. Not even Davey could criticise that attitude.

Again that night Julia was the last to go to bed. She had gone down to Davey's cottage to feed the lamb and to see if Davey were in, and she had lingered on the way back because, apart from the sharp cold, it was a lovely night, the moon shining through drifting white clouds so that the patterned sky was a reflection of the snow-patterned ground. She would grow to love this place, Julia thought. The chill dominance of the mountains would no longer frighten her, and the loneliness of the sheep-sprinkled hills would become a friendly thing. She was determined to be happy.

It was as she came up the path beneath the trees to the front door that she saw the two figures, Davey and a strange woman.

Davey called to her. "Miss Paget, this is Miss Carmichael. Do you think she could have a bed for the night? Her car skidded and upset in a ditch."

The woman came forward. She was a stout little person full of bustle and apology.

"I'm not a bit hurt, Miss Paget, but this gentleman assures me nothing can be done about my car until daylight. I do so hate to be a trouble. Just a little dry corner anywhere where I can curl up will do splendidly. And please don't arouse the household. It's awfully late."

Julia thought quickly. The best thing to do would be to let Miss Carmichael have her room, and she could sleep on the couch downstairs, or in the little room where Timmy had spent his first night.

She opened the door and said welcomingly,

"You must be upset after an accident like that. Do come in."

"Just a little chilly," the woman admitted. "I was on my way to Mt. Cook. So annoying."

"I'll make you a hot drink," Julia offered. "Supposing I take you upstairs. I'll bring you a drink in bed. Davey—I think Lily has gone to bed. Then I won't need to disturb anybody."

When, a little later, she had settled the profusely apologetic lady in her room and had come downstairs, she found Davey had put out cups and made cocoa.

"Sorry about this," he said as she came in. "I couldn't leave the poor thing stranded."

"Of course you couldn't. I think I'll give her a couple of aspirins to settle her nerves. She's in a state of jitters."

"Don't go giving her your room," Davey said.

Julia was touched by his thoughtfulness. "Oh no, there's plenty of room," she said lightly. Then added, "Davey, where were you last night? Were you in here?"

He looked at her in some bewilderment. She noticed that his face was drawn with fatigue and that his eyelids were so heavy he almost had to prop them up with his fingers.

"In the kitchen? Last night? I may have been, at some stage. I can't remember."

"But you must remember!" she insisted impatiently. "It's important. Do you usually come in?"

"Yes, Lily makes me a drink if I'm not too late. But I don't think I came in last night. There were too many lambs dying in the snow. Honestly—it's silly—I don't think I can remember."

Julia wanted to shake him awake. It was too exasperating that when he might have had a simple answer to her problem Davey was too stupid with fatigue to give her one. Or was he simulating that extreme tiredness so as to avoid answering her question?

"Davey, there was someone out here and I must know who it was. It's important." (She couldn't say, "I know it's fantastic, but I must assure myself that Harry, who is dead, isn't in this house. I must be absolutely sure that Kate and Paul are telling the truth. Why should they lie? Why should they hide Harry? It doesn't make sense, but I must be *sure*.")

Davey gave her his blank stare. "If it was me," he said in his blurred voice, "I can assure you it wouldn't be Lily. She doesn't stay up till midnight for me."

The unspoken question was in Julia's eyes. Then for whom does Lily stay up until midnight? She couldn't say that either. She had already talked too much to Davey. If Lily had been accustomed to stay up for Paul, that was over now. She understood about that. But if it were, by some fantastic chance, Harry . . .

"The cocoa's getting cold," Davey said mildly.

Julia picked up a cup and hurried upstairs with it. Miss Carmichael, wrapped in the warm dressing-gown Julia had lent her, was prowling about the room.

"Thank you *so* much, dear," she said effusively. "I can't tell you how kind you are. But I'm devastated at your giving me your bed. I shouldn't sleep a wink, but I just know I'm going to." She yawned, and took the hot cocoa from Julia, and thanked her with extravagant repetition. At last Julia got out of the room. Davey *must* remember about last night, she was saying to herself as she hurried downstairs.

But Davey's dark head lay on the kitchen table. His eyes flickered open as Julia came in.

"Thanks—for feeding—the lamb," he murmured.

Julia stood over him helplessly.

"Davey, you can't sleep here." She stared at his unmoving head. It was awful to think he was going to sleep uncomfortably like that all night. She couldn't let him. She went into the living room and got a cushion which she tried to put under his head.

He stirred. "Don't worry. I can sleep anywhere. Be all right soon. The snow gets them. They die of cold." He was mumbling in his sleep. "Thanks—Queen of Sheba."

Julia crept away, full of remorse. She must tell Paul that he was working Davey to death. When the poor boy couldn't even remember whether or not he had come in for a hot drink the previous night it proved that he was shockingly tired. But *could* he remember? Davey's dark, watchful eyes were never quite readable.

Some time in the small hours of the morning Julia, chilly on the living-room couch, wondered what the exuberant Miss Carmichael would do if she found one of those charming little *billet-doux* under her door in the morning. Then she thought of Lily finding Davey asleep in the kitchen and she began to chuckle sleepily.

When, much later, after light had filtered through the drawn curtains, she heard the scream, she rolled tiredly off the couch, realising that Lily had found Davey. But there was no need for the silly girl to scream.

## TWELVE

"MR. BLAINE! Mr. Blaine! Help!"

That was Lily's hysterical voice, not from the kitchen but from upstairs.

"Miss Paget has fallen off the balcony!"

There were footsteps running upstairs, punctuated by Kate's distressed exclamations. Julia went to the front door and wrenching it open ran round the house, over the slippery patches of snow to the little plot of garden directly beneath her window. Almost before she was bending over the inert form of Miss Carmichael, still wrapped in her own pale-pink dressing-gown, Paul was there behind her, covering the ground in leaps and hops as he tried to move quickly on his lame foot. As Julia looked up she saw that Paul's face was quite white, his eyes starting with horror.

She said, "It's not me, darling. It's poor Miss Carmichael."

As she spoke Miss Carmichael stirred and moaned. Paul exclaimed in a loud voice of relief,

"Who the devil is Miss Carmichael? What's she doing falling off your balcony?"

Miss Carmichael's eyes opened. "The rail broke," she murmured. "Must have been rotten."

"Let's get her inside," Julia said. "I wonder if she's badly hurt."

Miss Carmichael, whose rosy face was drained of colour, but who was possessed of a hardy spirit, made another effort.

"It's just my shoulder, dear. I've wrenched it. Must have fainted, I think. Stupid of me." Her lips were white, but she managed a dim smile. "Seems as if I'm determined to kill myself."

Kate was calling from the balcony, where the broken wood hung drunkenly.

"Who *is* that woman?"

Lily was beside Julia, panting heavily, and Julia was momentarily conscious of Nita's thin white wedge of a face coming to peer over Kate's shoulder.

"She arrived late last night," Julia explained. "Her car had skidded and turned over. I didn't want to disturb anyone so I gave her my room."

Paul was helping Miss Carmichael to her feet. Lily, still panting, as if in distress or fear, supported her on the other side, and slowly they made their way indoors.

After that there was a great deal of fuss and bustle. Kate poured a generous brandy for Miss Carmichael who immediately became garrulous. Dove, whom Lily had run to fetch, said that in her opinion Miss Carmichael had suffered no injuries beyond her wrenched shoulder and shock.

"I only went out to look at the wonderful view," Miss Carmichael explained. "Those snow peaks are just glorious. I was leaning on the side of the balcony just gazing open-mouthed when suddenly I found myself falling."

"You might have been killed!" Kate declared.

"Well, it wasn't such a big fall as that. I suppose I could have broken my neck." She smiled cheerfully. "And after Miss Paget so kindly giving me her room, too. I guess there's a hoodoo on me at present."

Nita, who still looked haggard and white, as if she had slept badly, said in her soft significant way, "Miss Carmichael's bad luck seems to be your good luck, Julia. It might have happened to you."

And suddenly Julia remembered vidily the scene two mornings ago when Nita had found her on the balcony. Lily had come in with her tea, and Dove had looked up from the garden on her way home. She might have fallen that morning. She had leaned over the frail railing, watching Dove. Had the thought entered the mind of one of those three women that one day she might fall?

In the same instant she remembered going into her room the other night and seeing the long windows wide open, knowing that she had left them closed. . . .

Just as that shivery feeling of premonition more than dread came over her Davey came in. He was fully dressed and he looked alert and rested. His dark eyes surveyed the scene.

"Anything I can do?"

Paul answered, "We've had a bit of an accident. I'll drive Miss Carmichael into Timaru." He gave the protesting Miss Carmichael his charming generous smile. "I'm no use round here with a bad leg, and anyway I want to go to town again. Some business I didn't finish the other day."

Nita made a sudden step towards him, then stopped.

Paul said, "Would you like to change your mind, Nita, and come with me and bring Timmy."

As she dropped her eyelids her face became expressionless.

"No. I'd like to stay for the wedding if you don't mind."

106

"I don't mind," said Paul. He looked at Julia, but all she could manage, in that moment of suspicion and fear, was a frozen smile of assent. It was as if she were speaking the words herself when Davey said quite calmly,

"That balcony was pretty rotten, but I'm surprised it collapsed without a little help."

Paul's head shot up. "What do you mean?"

"Nothing at all. Merely an observation."

"Oh, but you don't realise how heavy I am," Miss Carmichael said gaily. "And I foolishly leaned my whole weight on the rail, mountain-gazing. I don't think you need be afraid that there was anything *sinister*. That would only happen in books. Perhaps that young man reads a lot of books."

"He writes 'em," said Paul.

"Well, there you are!"

Kate gave a sudden high giggle that was more than half a sob.

"Such a stupid accident. It's brought on my headache. I'm afraid I shall have to go back to bed. Oh dear, and there's Granny rapping. Would you run up to her, Julia, and explain that she can't come down yet."

"You look pale, dear. Have you had a fright? Has Harry been up to his tricks again?" the old lady said when Julia had done her best to explain the confusion downstairs. She sat up in bed, her chicken-leg wrists protruding from the wide sleeves of her nightgown, her head cocked alertly. "Sometimes I wonder if you should stay with Harry, dear. He's my own grandson, but I do know that he has made a number of women unhappy. And you look a sensitive little thing. You will have to grow a thick skin if you stay here."

"Granny why would someone play tricks with the balcony so I would fall off it?" Julia demanded distressfully.

"Good gracious!" exclaimed the old lady. "What a daring thing to do. Now that must be quite Harry's most naughty prank. Why, it's even dangerous!"

Julia sighed hopelessly. She was beginning to agree with Paul that Georgina was crazy all the time even when she seemed lucid. But she did realise the balcony trick—if it

107

were a trick—was dangerous. Anonymous letters could be disturbing, salt in one's tea and moths in the bedroom were also distressing and hurtful tricks. But if someone had deliberately weakened the railing of the balcony it was certainly dangerous.

It was not likely, of course, that she would have been killed. She would have been hurt and badly frightened. Perhaps she would have gone away, leaving Paul . . .

When she went into her room and out on to the damaged balcony she saw Davey down in the snow. He had a fragment of the broken railing in his hand.

She peered over. "Well?" she asked breathlessly.

"Someone could have been messing around with a saw," he said. Then he looked up at her with calm deliberation, and as if his voice were saying those words again she heard quite clearly what he had said last night. "Don't go giving her your room." Just like that. "Don't go giving her your room because it might be dangerous. She might be the one to fall off the balcony and we don't want that to happen. . . ."

No, no! Not Davey! Davey had nothing to do with this dastardly trick. Julia looked down at him beseechingly.

"But they haven't?"

"It's hard to tell. The wood's splintered now." He carelessly tossed the piece of railing away.

Julia suddenly called, "Davey, wait there. I'm coming down." When she got there she said to Davey, "What made you look to see if the balcony had been interfered with?"

He gave his small smile. "My mind works that way."

She seized his arm demanding, "Is it only because you have a mind like that? Or is there something queer here? Something apart from jealous women? Something—like—a man who is supposed to be dead. . . ."

"It would be difficult to trace the record of a death in Australia from here," he remarked.

She was suddenly holding her breath, full of that familiar dread.

"Davey, even if Harry is alive—why should I be frightened? What's it to do with me?"

"Perhaps Australia was convenient," he said to himself.

"You mean, so that I can't make enquiries? But there's

Nita, so unhappy, there's Kate who weeps if you mention Harry." She swept her arm, indicating the tall old house. "Could anyone be living here and never be seen?"

She thought of the times when she had so nearly come upon someone unexpectedly, the other night in the kitchen when someone had thrust her out, the hollows in the two pillows on Nita's bed, the unexplained whispering and laughter she had heard. A sudden idea came to her. "If Harry is here he must eat. Lily will tell me."

"What will Lily tell you?" That was Paul's voice behind them. He had suddenly appeared and although his voice was pleasant his eyes had a chilly look that Julia had not seen before. She realised that he did not like her questioning his servants.

"How many people she cooks for," she said stubbornly. Paul's fair brows drew together.

"Julia, once and for all, will you stop imagining these preposterous things." He suddenly seemed to realise that Davey was listening, and he tried to control the impatience in his voice. "Look here, Davey," he said, "you and Julia might have similar imaginations, but I rather resent you airing them openly. I can't have people going around saying traps are being set in my house to hurt people. Damn it, it isn't funny! You keep that sort of thing for your books."

"I don't write that sort of book," Davey said mildly.

As he went away Paul said, frowning, "He's an odd chap. Because I made him a friend he thinks he can say what he likes. I'm inclined to think I was a bit rash in bringing him up here."

"Because he's concerned about my welfare?" Julia asked swiftly.

"Your welfare?"

"Don't be so blind, Paul! Don't you realise that I was the one who should have fallen off that balcony? That's what Davey has been thinking."

"He's got to mind his own business!" Paul shouted. "The whole thing was an accident. That railing was rotten. Anyway, it might never have broken with your weight. You could probably have leaned over it for the next ten years with perfect safety. Miss Carmichael is a big woman. Why did you give her your bedroom, anyway? Why didn't you wake Mother? You didn't have to sleep on the couch all night. It was a crazy thing to do."

Julia looked at his heated face.

"Paul, you're upset."

"And why shouldn't I be?" he demanded in his strained, angry voice. "Do I need Davey to remind me that you might have fallen off that balcony? Good God, don't you know yet that I love you!"

Strangely enough, after it was all over and Paul had left for Timaru with the shaken but valiantly cheerful Miss Carmichael, Julia realised that it was Paul's attitude that had distressed her the most.

She thought back over his behaviour since her arrival. First there was his casualness about having her met in Timaru, then his failure to recognise her when she arrived. After that there was his confident but light-hearted love-making, almost the kind that she would have expected him to make carelessly to Dove or Lily. But in the last day or two that had changed. He was no longer light-hearted with her. He tried to adopt his casual confident air, but underneath it he was deadly serious, almost as if he thought someone were trying to take her from him. It was clear that there was something worrying him. But what was it, and why didn't he tell her? It was stupid to have secrets. It not only worried but frightened her. There was something queerly frightening about Paul's attitude. When he held her in his arms there was a ruthlessness about his action as if he thought she would be snatched away.

No doubt his illness was to blame. But she couldn't help secretly regretting the gay light-hearted Paul of the first days of her arrival, and even the sober shy person she had known in England. There was something of the chameleon about him. He took colour from the events that pleased or distressed him. Now he was behaving like a desperate man resolved on getting his own way. But what had happened to make him fear his plans would be upset?

*Was it Harry?*

Paul planned to stay overnight in Timaru. There was business he wanted to finalise and by the time that was done it would be too late to begin the long drive back. So the house was occupied only by women again.

And now the undercurrents were even more apparent. Kate said the shock of Miss Carmichael's accident had brought on her headache so badly that she was going to stay in her room all day. Her eyes seemed paler and a little protuberant. She hadn't been equipped by nature to cope with unpleasant emergencies and her instinct was to run away. That was obvious. But she couldn't run away from Heriot Hills so she could do nothing but take refuge in bed with numerous cups of tea and sweet biscuits.

But Nita didn't want to hide from anything. Her face wore the strangest expression. It was so unusual to associate pity with Nita's gleaming contemptuous eyes that it was not for a little while that Julia recognised that emotion. Then it made her intensely uncomfortable.

Nita seemed to be constantly at her elbow, watching her, saying little significant things in her husky voice.

"Don't you feel just a little shaky after all that? I'm sure I should."

"Why?" said Julia coldly. "It wasn't I who fell."

"No, but it so nearly was. And you're not so well padded as Miss Carmichael. You might easily have broken bones." She looked at Julia with her narrowed eyes. "You might have been seriously injured."

Then a little later she said, "Of course it wasn't very tactful of Davey to suggest the balcony might have been tampered with, although it's the thought that leaps to the mind."

"Who would tamper with it?" Julia asked calmly.

"How should I know? But someone does seem to have been playing tricks on you."

Julia darted her a quick look. Did she know about the letters?

Nita fluttered her bony little hands that were like shells covered with pale brown skin.

"Well, you were the one to say it when you found those moths in your room," she said. "But they were harmless, by comparison."

With an effort Julia kept her temper.

"The wood of the balcony was rotten," she insisted. "Paul said so and he knows. Just to prove it, come and we'll try the other two balconies and see what happens."

Nita was nervous, or pretended to be so. When Julia recklessly leaned hard against the railing of the balcony leading from Georgina's room she cried, "Don't do it. You'll kill yourself." But when the railing proved to be quite firm the look of sly pity came back into her eyes.

"You see, that one is perfectly safe," she said.

It was Kate, huddled under the eiderdown, the colour unnaturally high in her cheeks, who protested agitatedly as Julia tested the balcony leading from that room.

"Don't go out there!" she cried. "I shall never set foot on one of those treacherous things again."

The railing creaked ominously. Julia found that it gave to the pressure of her body. She drew back, and said triumphantly, "It's rotten, just as I said. This one would break even with my weight. Kate, we must get the balconies strengthened or taken down."

Nita refused to be baulked of her triumph.

"I shouldn't bother, if I were you. I should refuse to live in such a dangerous house." Her gleaming eyes sought Kate. "Don't you agree, Kate? Isn't it better to be too suspicious than not suspicious enough?"

Kate burrowed further under the eiderdown.

"If you think the house is so dangerous, Nita dear, there's no need for you to stay."

"Oh, I shall stay," Nita said. "If only to protect Julia."

The idea of needing protection was ironic enough, but the idea of Nita being the one to give it to her was even more ironic. But perhaps she had misjudged the girl. The half-ashamed friendliness she had recognised once or twice must exist more strongly beneath her hostility than Julia had thought. Nita might be deriving a morbid excitement from the events, but she also seemed sincerely concerned about them.

"Really," she insisted, "I'd think twice before I'd agree to live here. Horrid, damp, tumbledown old place. Thank goodness Harry never brought me here."

"Then he used to come here," Julia said softly.

Unexpectedly the colour flamed in Nita's thin face. She dropped her eyelids, but not before Julia had seen the flash of excitement in her eyes.

"Oh, long ago," she said carelessly. "As a boy. That's why Granny is always talking about him."

"Not since?"

"Not since we were married."

"But Granny always speaks of him as an adult. As if," said Julia slowly, "she had known him a very short time ago." When Nita didn't speak she went on, "Very old people often don't remember much about their middle years. It's their childhood and very recent things that stay in their mind. One would think that she remembered Harry from quite recently."

She was meditating and was quite unprepared for Nita's flinging round on her, her face flaming with anger.

"You're trying to suggest that Harry left me! Well, he didn't. You're quite wrong. He never left me to come here. He never left me at all. We loved each other. We were man and wife—always." She lingered over the last word, and then said it again, with a peculiar finality, "Always. So just stop talking about him, will you? Because I can't stand it."

Julia was silent a moment, filled with pity. There was no mistaking now the torment in Nita's face. She would not shed tears of grief, she would be flamingly angry always.

"I'm sorry," she said sincerely. "It's you, Nita, who shouldn't stay here. It's too hard for you, seeing Paul and I happy when you are left like this."

But Nita had recovered and was her familiar acid self.

"Oh, I wouldn't grudge you *Paul*," she said. She placed emphasis on the name, and the look of mocking amusement was back in her eyes. Julia began to wonder if she were quite normal.

But in face of all that it just wasn't feasible to imagine that Harry was somehow secretly living at Heriot Hills.

The situation was quite simple. One of the women here was in love with Paul and was being vindictive. As a result there were the letters, the salt in her tea, the moths which she violently hated in her bedroom. All of these things were harmless and intended to be harmless. The broken railing of the balcony was a genuine accident. Paul's tense behaviour was that of a nervous bridegroom. Nita was desperately unhappy because Paul and Julia reminded her

113

of what she had lost. Davey, being a writer, had a too highly developed imagination. Kate got fussed and upset too easily, and Georgina's mind was one long fairy-tale.

That was how things were. There was nothing to be seriously concerned about. It would be satisfactory to find out whether Dove or Lily was the author of the letters, but even that was not important. This morning there had been none, so the writer must have decided to give them up.

(But this morning the balcony had collapsed, and no one but Julia had known there was a stranger sleeping in her room.)

Julia resolutely put the niggling thought from her. There was nothing to worry about. Nothing at all.

Then she discovered that the pearls Paul had brought her from Timaru were missing.

She knew that she had not mislaid them, because although the contents of the drawer in which she had put them were still tidy they were faintly disturbed, enough to show that someone had most carefully been searching among them.

It was too bad! This last discovery made Julia want to sit down and weep. Was she never going to be allowed to have any peace? Why did someone hate her so much?

She pressed her hands to her forehead and forced herself to think logically. Whoever had taken the pearls might have done so out of malice, but could not the reason also have been greed? The pearls were beautiful, and of sufficient value to tempt a thief. Who was likely to be a thief in this house?

Instantly, perhaps unfairly, Julia's thoughts turned to Lily. She was the one who had the easiest access to the room. She came in to tidy and make the bed. She knew Paul had given Julia the pearls. She may have been jealous, or she may genuinely have wanted to own them. It would be foolish and dangerous to steal things from her future mistress, but she might have succumbed to a sudden temptation.

On the other hand Miss Carmichael, whom no one knew anything about, had spent the night in this room. What was to prevent her from prowling inquisitively among Julia's possessions and being tempted.

But one could not associate thieving with Miss Carmichael's open determinedly cheerful face.

What about Dove Robinson? There had been a great deal of confusion in the house after Miss Carmichael's fall. Anyone could have slipped up unnoticed to Julia's room.

Even Georgina, in her fumbling absent-minded way, could have prowled. Or Nita, who was so strung-up with her secret emotions, and could have had her own reasons for depriving Julia of a beautiful present.

Or was the thief someone she had never met, someone who lived here and was never seen. . . .

Julia began to shiver. She longed for Paul to come back. She began to dread the long hours until tomorrow afternoon when he would return. Anything might happen, she thought nervously. There might be just some petty upset, or the person who had wanted her to fall off the balcony and who had been thwarted might try another method.

No, no, no! She mustn't think such unmitigated nonsense. No one wanted her to die, not even a crazily jealous woman.

But perhaps there could be just a little accident that would remove her from the household. . . .

She was not thinking coherently. The uncomfortable night on the couch downstairs, and all the subsequent upsets had made her too tired to think intelligently. But if these crazy ideas were going to continue niggling at her there was only one thing to do, and that was to sit up all night. Then no marauder or mischief-maker could catch her unawares.

# THIRTEEN

AT half-past ten Julia took all the folded scraps of paper, like little serpents, out of their hiding place in her jewel box, and spread them out on the bed.

When, just before dinner, she had gone down to Davey's cottage to feed the lamb which was now tethered to an old dog kennel at the back door, she had found a sheet of manuscript paper lying carelessly but ostentatiously on Davey's desk. On it was written—*Are you sure you love him? Are you quite sure? Think very well about it. Even if you are just a little in doubt, you can depend that it is not love you feel for him.*

It was a part of Davey's book, of course. He had stopped at that point before going out on his duties as a shepherd. It wasn't even very good, Julia thought regretfully. No one talked quite like that in real life. It had a flavour of melodrama.

However, events in real life sometimes had a flavour of melodrama, also. These anonymous letters spread out on the bed were not part of any book, good or bad. They had really happened. They had not been left lying ostentatiously on a desk to catch her eye, so that she could attribute them to herself if she wished, but had been thrust at her, most deliberately.

*Think well before you marry Paul Blaine. . . . Paul Blaine is no good for you. . . . You will never wear that beautiful dress to marry Paul Blaine. . . .*

The thick black lettering bore no relation to Davey's fine upright hand, yet queerly the notes seemed to be all part of the same thing. *Are you sure you love him? Think very well about it. . . .*

Julia's head was spinning. She thought she could hear voices saying the malicious words, chanting them over and over. It was only the wind, of course, and the occasional lost bleating of a lamb. The branches of the silver poplars, with their flickering white leaves, rustled constantly. The night was full of loneliness.

If she truly loved Paul would she find his home so lonely? Julia sat in the middle of the floor, propping her back which ached with weariness against the end of the bed, and thought back over her acquaintance with Paul. There was the first time he had come to Uncle Jonathan's house, a shy young soldier, lonely and a long way from home. He said his grandmother had told him to come, and he had been grateful for hospitality. Julia remembered how Uncle Jonathan, who had been the strictest of guardians in so far as her friendships with boys had been concerned, had almost thrust her in Paul's arms. But he had been fair. If he had always remembered that Paul was his beloved Georgina's grandson he had also formed the highest opinion of Paul's character. He had given Julia complete freedom and made no comment on the hours she kept. He didn't keep reminding her, in his slightly acid way as he generally did, that she was only nineteen and at that age a kiss was likely to seem binding for life. Indeed, he had looked as if he expected Paul's kisses to be exactly that.

But Julia, trying to remember her exact sensations at that first rather inexpert kiss of Paul's, knew she hadn't experienced anything but a shy pleasure. None of the tumultuous feelings Uncle Jonathan had seemed to expect had swept through her. Rather, they had come when Paul, after his long silence, had begun writing to her again.

Their love was based on a slender beginning. If Paul had not written to her with such beautiful and sensitive intimacy they would have met virtually as strangers. Her deep delight in his letters combined with the fact of his illness had swept away any surprise that he should have kept such ardent feelings secret for so long.

Now she had no doubt about Paul's passionate sincerity. But she herself—was she in love with a dream?

"Paul, I want you here near me!" she whispered. "Now. Show me I love you."

Outside the trees rustled with a never-ceasing sound. Inside there was only the faint creaking of old tired walls.

Tomorrow when Paul came back she would tell him about the loss of her pearls. She had deliberately kept silence today, for what was the use of making more trouble? No one would tell her the truth. Kate would get hysterical, and Nita would smile in that curious pitying way as she had done all day. Georgina would blame the mythical Harry, and as for Lily—was it chance or insolence that had caused her to wear a small fine string of pearls that evening. She had said she was going over to Dove Robinson's to play cards. There was no love lost between her and Dove, but one had to do something in the depths of the country. That remark had been made in response to Julia's polite question as to why Lily was dressed up, her body slim but richly curved in a pale-blue sweater and skirt. When Julia pursued the topic by asking Lily if she liked living in the country she got the enigmatic answer, "Not as much as I thought I would." And with that she had had to be contented.

Had Lily's pleasure been spoilt by her arrival? That, obviously, was the implication.

Julia sighed unhappily. It was horrid to be so disliked, and through no fault of her own. She got up from her cramped position on the floor and went indifferently to the mirror. "Why, you're a pretty thing!" she thought she could hear Paul's surprised voice, as she looked at her dark tousled hair, her shadowed eyes, her cheeks hollowed with strain. Hadn't Paul thought she was pretty when he had first known her, she wondered tiredly. In a few days, under these conditions, she would no longer look like anything. She would go to her wedding a sunken-eyed ghost.

Listlessly she picked up her hair brush. She ought to take more interest in her appearance. She could begin now by giving her hair a hundred strokes. Of course, it would scarcely matter if her hair were brushed or unbrushed supposing some accident befell her. . . .

A sudden gust of wind made the whole house tremble. It died away, like waves receding on sand, then rose again, more strongly. At the same instant, as the house shuddered with the wind, there was a sound like a door closing.

Julia softly put down the brush. She tiptoed to her door and endeavoured to open it without a sound. She looked

118

down the stairs into the dark hallway. The wind rose to a thin shriek. It sounded almost like high laughter. The curtains in the room behind her billowed out, although the long windows were closed. There was silence downstairs. No one stirred. It must have been her imagination that a door had closed.

That was when the idea came to her to give Lily's room a quick search and see if she could find the missing pearls. It was unlikely that Lily would be home before midnight. If she did come in unexpectedly Julia could make some excuse about looking for aspirin or something. That would not be good, but it was worth taking the risk to get at, perhaps, some of the truth.

Lily slept in a downstairs room off the passage to the kitchen. The door was standing wide open, proof that Lily had not yet returned home. Julia, using a flashlight, went in softly and shone the light on Lily's neat narrow bed, on the old-fashioned dresser, of a piece with all the massive furniture in the house, the wardrobe, and the low dressing-table on which was a clutter of toilet accessories.

The most likely place in which to find the pearls would be the drawers of the dressing-table. Feeling rather ashamed of herself Julia pulled out the top drawer. It was sparsely filled with Lily's possessions, handkerchiefs, gloves, and nylon stockings. The next drawer held a quantity of very filmy and delicate underclothing including a black nylon night-dress. How would Lily, who had come to Heriot Hills as a servant in the house, have imagined that she would have any use for those very dainty things? There could be only one answer to that. She must have cherished hopes of one day, and in the very near future, being something more than a servant.

Julia felt the hot colour of embarrassment and pity in her cheeks. Poor simple Lily! What had that naughty Paul led her to believe? There seemed little doubt now as to who was the author of the notes. Lily was fighting a hopeless but defiant rearguard action. But what was this? It was a small square piece of paper, and on it was written in scrawling handwriting, *Dear Lily, I would like you to have this. Nita.*

Julia stared at the contents of the drawer. What article

had Nita given Lily? The nightdress? The silk negligée? The lacy panties? And why had she felt the impulse to give Lily a present? She had been here only a few days. Lily could not have rendered her any particular service. Or had she? Was it that Nita felt it wise to keep in Lily's good graces?

Still staring, another scrap of paper caught Julia's eye. It was a cutting from a newspaper, folded in half and lying in the bottom of the drawer as if it had fallen from among her clothing when she unpacked. Julia picked it up and shone the light on it. It was a clipping from the social column of some woman's magazine. It read, rather coyly,

It is with great interest that we learn that the fine old homestead, Heriot Hills, fallen into disrepair since the death of Mr. Adam Blaine, is to be restored to its former importance. Mrs. Blaine's elder grandson who has been abroad for some years arrived last week, and there are rumours of wedding plans. Who is the lucky bride? That is still a deep secret, but after a glimpse of Mr. Blaine we predict there will be flutters in many feminine breasts.

Obviously, thought Julia, the cunning Lily had laid her plans. She had thought it would be fun to keep house for a bachelor, not knowing that the bachelor status was extremely temporary. She must have fallen in love with Paul during that first interview with him. No wonder Julia's arrival had been so upsetting to her. She had taken a week off to shadow Julia and try to frighten her away. But she had not succeeded. Probably at this moment she was thinking that she had only a few days in which to succeed. Poor Lily, with her seductive clothing, her forlorn hopes. . . .

Julia tried to think coherently. The main thing was to complete her search for the pearls. Lily would be home at any time and it would be humiliating to be caught in her room. Where would she be likely to hide a small flat box? Under the mattress? Julia turned to the bed to life the coverings. At the same instant the scream sounded.

*"Harry!"*

The scream was followed, a moment later, by a thud, like

someone falling. Almost instantly there was a loud shriek, this time the terror in it so intense that Julia instinctively clapped her hands to her ears.

Then she came to life. The screams had seemed to come from downstairs somewhere towards the front of the house. Someone was in extreme trouble with the mysterious Harry. At last, she thought, as she ran along the passage, she was going to encounter this elusive person.

Half way down the passage she smelt smoke. There seemed to be a faint chink of light coming under the library door. That, too, was where the smell of smoke came from. As Julia reached the door she heard running footsteps upstairs, and Kate's high shrill voice calling, "What's the matter? Who screamed?"

She flung open the library door and saw, in the firelight, the figure lying on the floor. There was a strong odour of burnt material. There was no one in the room but the figure on the floor.

Julia switched on the light and with a little cry bent over Nita. Nita's eyes flickered open. "Pushed me," she muttered.

"Who pushed you?" Julia asked. Then she saw that the filmy stuff of Nita's nightgown, which was her only garment, was burnt in a ragged line from top to bottom, and that little spirals of smoke still came from the rug on which Nita was lying. The fire in the grate smouldered redly.

"Nita!" Julia said urgently. "Was it Harry?"

She should be running for help. Nita's leg and hands were painfully burnt, and the girl herself was on the verge of unconsciousness. But Julia had to get an answer to her question.

"Was it Harry who pushed you? Nita!"

Nita's lips moved. She gave a low moan, full, it seemed to Julia, of the bitterest disillusionment. Was it in assent? Julia was certain it was. Then her eyes closed and she lost consciousness.

At the same moment Kate was there, her wrap flowing about her, her blonde hair wrapped in curling pins.

"Whatever has happened? Is somebody ill?" She came closer, and gave a small scream, instantly stifling it with her fingers bitten between her teeth. "It's Nita!"

"She's burnt," said Julia. "Her nightgown caught on fire.

121

She rolled herself on the floor. We must get Dove. These burns may be serious."

Kate leaned closer to look at Nita's unconscious face. Then she began to moan. "Oh, my goodness, what next? Whatever next?"

Later, thought Julia, with the calm part of her mind, she would remember Kate's words and think of the terror and apprehension in them. Just now there was no time to think.

"I'll go and get Dove. And Davey, too. You stay with Nita. Try to give her a little brandy if she comes round." She saw Kate's protruding eyes, with their naked look of fear. "You're not scared to stay, are you?"

Kate's breath came unevenly.

"It's such a shock. How could she get burnt? It's these inflammable materials girls wear nowadays. She shouldn't have been near a fire in that nightgown."

"She said she was pushed," Julia stated deliberately, and at the same moment, for the first time, she noticed that the window of the library was open, wide open, as if someone might have escaped that way.

"*Pushed!*" whispered Kate. She seemed to shrink inside her pretty frivolous gown, like a doll losing its stuffing. Then she sank in a flurry of silks and laces beside the unconscious Nita.

# FOURTEEN

AFTERWARDS, Julia told Davey that it was like the stage in the last act of a Shakespearean tragedy, Nita unconscious and Kate tumbled beside her, in almost as dire a condition.

But that was a very long time afterwards. It seemed like a whole night and a day, although it was only little more than five hours. There had been the frantic waiting for the doctor, who had come a ten-mile journey across the valley, while Dove watched by the unconscious Nita, and Julia

122

vainly tried to soothe Kate's hysterics. Then, on the doctor's insistence, there had been the nightmare trip to Timaru where it was urgent that Nita should be put in a hospital at once. Since Paul was away they had had to borrow the doctor's car. Davey had driven, and Julia had sat in the back, supporting Nita's sagging figure as comfortably as possible. She thought that the narrow dark shape of Davey's head against the windscreen would remain in her memory for ever. That, and the dead weight of Nita's shoulders and head against her. An entire lifetime had seemed to go by. There was nothing in the world but the curving hills against the blanched sky, the road winding and winding, the headlights of the car spotlighting clumps of trees, an isolated group of farm buildings, a black shining stream. And Davey's dark immovable head against the windscreen.

There was no memory and no future. Nothing existed but the turning, turning motion of the car, dizzily following the winding road, and the ache of her arms under Nita's weight. Everything was physical. She could neither think nor be afraid.

But when the fear came, later, it was overwhelming.

This was no simple, easily explained accident like Miss Carmichael's. This had been a deliberate attack. All the time, when she had thought the enemy was hers, it had been Nita who had been in danger. Someone had wanted to kill Nita.

How could she go back to a house in which lived a potential murderer?

At the hospital they said it was a miracle that Nita had not suffered more extensive burns. If she had not had the presence of mind to roll herself on the floor instantly she would have been badly if not fatally burnt. As it was, only one thigh and her hands were affected. The serious thing was the shock from which she was suffering. Although she had recovered consciousness before Julia left her she did not seem to recognise either Julia or Davey, and was indifferent to her surroundings.

Julia bent over her and tried to arouse a spark of recognition in the dark, narrow eyes that, having lost their gipsy sparkle, were peculiarly unfamiliar and frightening.

"Nita, if you could just remember! It's so important. Were you pushed into the fire?"

Nita's face was white, unalive.

"Nita, if it was Harry who pushed you, why did he? Why?"

The nurse took Julia's arm.

"It's no use, dear. She can't remember what happened. The shock has made her lose her memory."

"Temporarily?" Julia asked, as she let the nurse lead her away from Julia's bedside.

"Well, we hope so. Although I've seen cases where they never get it back. You'd better talk to the doctor."

Davey was waiting outside. He took Julia's arm and said in a matter-of-fact voice, "Now we'll have some breakfast."

"I didn't know it was morning," Julia said tiredly.

"No night lasts for ever."

"Davey—please, no cryptic remarks."

"A simple statement of fact. Where would you like to eat? Or would you like to go straight to Paul? He'll be at the George, I should think."

Julia instinctively shrank back.

"No," she said, rather breathlessly. "I don't want to see Paul just now."

She was not too tired to observe that the mocking look had gone out of Davey's eyes, and that his long narrow face held concern, and some other emotion. But her weariness did not allow her to interpret that other emotion. It might have been anger or it might have been a reluctant delight. His eyes were very bright.

"Then let's find somewhere to eat," he said.

He took her arm and they went down the quiet early morning street. The sea, stirring lazily, was beginning to take on the deepened colours of bright daylight. A train was puffing clouds of smoke down at the railway station, and the disturbed seabirds were wheeling and shrieking. Julia held out her hand and let the sun fall on it. The faint warmth, not quite dispersed in the frosty air, pleased her. Her other hand, tucked in Davey's arm, was warm, too. Gradually as she walked that dreadful cold feeling would go out of her body. The sea looked nice, sparkling and growing a deeper blue. When one looked to the northwest there were only the red-roofed houses growing tier by tier over the low hills. The mountains with their high, frozen dominance were shut out.

One had to cling to the thought of simple things, the frosty air, the immediate prospect of hot coffee, the difficulty of keeping her balance because the pavement was still slippery with frost and her legs were peculiarly weak at the knees.

They found a café down near the railway station that served tea or coffee and toast to early morning workers or men going off night shifts at the wharf. Davey said it wasn't very brilliant, but Julia said it was better than going to an hotel, looking like a waif. The coffee, surprisingly, was very good. Almost at once Julia's spirits began to lighten and her plans began to take form.

"Davey," she said, speaking quickly, "I'm not going back to Heriot Hills. It's impossible now. I should never want to see that house again. I couldn't be happy in it, after the things that have happened."

She lifted her eyes to look at him, and saw again that brightness in his own, as of some feeling that he was trying to suppress.

"Are you sure of this?" he asked.

"Of course I'm sure," she answered, rather acidly. "How do you think I could live there now. All the time I would be hearing Nita scream." A brief shudder went over her. She drew her breath and said firmly, "But it's not only Nita. There are other things. I haven't told you all of them. There's no point in going into them now, since I'm not going back. The thing's over and done with." For a moment she thought of Kate cowering in bed, a silly befrilled ostrich with her head in the sand, of Georgina muttering her litany about Harry and his mad dangerous pranks, of Dove and Lily whispering in the kitchen. "No," she said, "I couldn't go back."

She waited for Davey's inevitable question. Then, because she didn't want to hear it, she said quickly, "You took me there and now you've brought me back. It's like the end of a cycle."

But the question came, of course.

"Then you don't love Paul?"

125

She had known he was going to say that, yet she still had no answer ready. The whole thing was so painful and confused, and she had been trying to put it out of her mind, and pretend it had never happened.

"It's not that at all," she said. "Of course I love Paul. But every time I think of those horrible letters under my door, and Miss Carmichael falling off the balcony, and the moths that night. And I hear Nita scream." A wave of cold trembling went over her. She clenched her hands. "I do love Paul," she said desperately, "but he's in the middle of a nightmare. If I go back to him I'll have to be in that nightmare, too. I can't do it. Davey, I can't do it!"

He said nothing but, "Drink your coffee. I'll get some more."

After a few minutes the thing was in the back of her mind again, like a spider in a crevice. One knew it was there, but, gratefully, one could neither see nor feel it.

"Even my pearls," she said vaguely, "were stolen. Now who would do that?"

"Drink your coffee," said Davey.

"It would be Nita who was hiding Harry," Julia went on. "I know that, because of those two hollows in her pillow one morning. Someone had been with her, although she lied about it. And one night I heard him talking in the kitchen. I think probably he wrote those letters to me, too, or he made Nita write them. There must be some reason why he doesn't want me in the house, and particularly not to marry Paul. But I can't possibly think why."

Davey looked at her over the rim of his cup.

"If Harry is in the house, why should he hide?"

"Why should they tell me he is dead?" Julia flashed. "None of it makes sense." She caught Davey's look and said, "You don't believe he is really there, do you?"

"I find it difficult to believe that he could so consistently keep out of sight."

"It's a big house. He could. Davey, I'm sure he's there. Georgina knows. She's not wandering all the time. And Nita doesn't look like a widow. She's unhappy, but she doesn't look bereaved." She added flatly, "Well, someone pushed Nita last night. Who could it have been but Harry?"

126

The waitress was at their table saying in tired early morning voice, "More coffee?"

Julia shook her head. Davey produced money and paid the waitress. She went away, and Davey said, "When Nita can tell us what happened it will be quite simple."

"But supposing she has lost her memory forever. The nurse said it could happen, with a bad shock. And it was a dreadful shock Nita got. How would you feel if someone you loved suddenly tried to kill you?"

David said briskly, "Even if you don't want to see Paul, we must let him know what has happened."

"Yes, I suppose so," Julia agreed, shutting her mind against the memory of Paul with his choir-boy face that might or might not hide knowledge of the fact that his brother was in the house. "Telephone him from here, can you? Don't say I'm here. There'll be time for that later. I can't argue now. I couldn't face it."

All the time Davey was in the booth telephoning she thought of the wedding dress shut in the dark room-sized wardrobe at Heriot Hills. Poor lovely dress. It was becoming as much a ghost as Harry Blaine and his peculiar, deadly haunting of the house. Uncle Jonathan would be so disappointed. It was going to be very hard telling him what she had decided.

Presently Davey came back, looking puzzled.

"Paul isn't at the George," he said.

"He's left?"

"No, he didn't stay there last night, they say."

"Then he's somewhere else." Julia sighed. "Do we have to try every hotel in the town?"

"My guess is that it wouldn't be much use. He'll probably have left for home by now."

"Then we can't see him." Julia's reaction to that was one of tired relief. She couldn't have borne Paul's eager eyes or his hands on her at that moment. She longed to stay in this state of passive indifference. It was so much easier.

The waitress was looking at them again. Obviously she wanted to clear the table. Suddenly Julia realised that she had no possessions and no place in the world to go. It was a completely new sensation and it startled her into full consciousness.

"Davey," she said in embarrassment, "can you lend me some money?"

"Of course. I'll give you what I have with me." He promptly began to turn out his pockets, and tumbled on to the table three crumpled pound notes and a miscellany of silver and coppers. Julia began to count it carefully. "So I'll know what I owe you," she said. "There's four pounds two shillings and sevenpence here."

"That won't take you far, I'm afraid."

"It will do until I hear from Uncle Jonathan. I'll cable him today."

"What do you plan to do in the meantime?"

"Stay here. I can't walk out on Nita. It's just that I won't go back to that house. As soon as Nita's all right and Uncle Jonathan sends me some money—well, I guess I'll go back to England."

All at once she felt inexplicably dreary at the thought of going home, all her high hopes destroyed. Tears began to tremble on her eyelids. She talked quickly, to keep her self-control.

"I'll book a room at the George. If we stay here any longer we're liable to be thrown out."

Davey stood up. "What about luggage?" he said in his matter-of-fact voice.

"Oh!" Julia, gathering up the little pile of money on the table, suddenly began to giggle. "This situation is a little compromising, but I'm afraid I'll have to buy a nightdress and toothbrush out of this. Come along, let's go to Woolworth's."

An hour later, standing in the lobby of the George Hotel, Julia was still inclined to giggle. The suitcase she carried was a cheap fibre one, and it held the modest total of her immediate requirements, a sprigged cotton nightdress, a toothbrush, a cake of soap and face flannel, and a couple of handkerchiefs.

"I'm sorry I didn't have more cash with me," Davey whispered to her.

"What did you think I wanted? Black chiffon?"

"What did you get?"

"Pale blue cotton with rosebuds. Juvenile but sweet."

Davey nodded approvingly.

"You didn't like the Queen of Sheba much, did you?" she said.

"Miscast," he answered in his brief manner.

The girl who came to the desk was the same languid person who had given Julia the anonymous letter a week ago. If she had taken notice of that letter would Nita Blaine have been desperately ill in hospital today? It was no use thinking of those things. Resolutely she clung to the frail and unexpected sweetness of buying the cheap nightdress with Davey's money.

Davey, in his businesslike and completely unruffled manner, arranged for her room, and then taking her aside said, "I suggest you put on that juvenile garment right away and get some sleep. I'll come back and have dinner with you this evening."

It was suddenly terrible to be left alone.

"Oh no! I couldn't sleep. I must go back to the hospital."

"You'll sleep," said Davey. "I'll go up to the hospital, and I'll telephone Heriot Hills and do a few other things. Now be a good girl."

"Davey, don't tell Paul."

He looked at her with his mocking eyes.

"Do you want to change your mind?"

"No, I can't go back. But I can't face him just now, either." And then, because Paul's face, hurt and vulnerable, rose before her, she was weeping. The tears were rolling down her cheeks in the completely uninhibited manner of her childhood when she had suddenly been lonely and lost in some red-carpeted seaside hotel. Davey took her arm and whisked her across the lounge, with its turkey-red carpet, its palms and its curiously staring occupants, and up the stairs.

He opened the door of her room and ushered her in. He put the cheap suitcase on the floor, and sat her on the edge of the bed and took out his handkerchief and wiped the tears off her cheeks. His face had a tender and completely competent look, as if he had frequently dried the tears of little girls. That was what he thought he was doing, she realised in humiliation, comforting a distressed child. Her lips trembled again. She had never cried in front of a man

129

before, and now she could not stop. He was treating her like a child and that was making her a child.

"Go away!" she wailed, and contrarily put out her hand to hold him.

His response was swift and utterly unexpected. He stooped and kissed her on her trembling lips.

She clung to him, then pushed him away. Confused emotions threatened to overcome her.

"I love Paul, Davey. Paul."

"So you do," he said calmly, indifferently. "Well, get into bed and get some sleep."

The door closed behind him. Julia, sitting quite still and composed, tried to remember his kiss. It had been to comfort a child. But it had comforted her, an adult person, composed and mature again. That was the peculiar thing about it.

She slept as Davey had told her to, and when she awoke late in the afternoon that composure remained with her. She began to think, almost with a thread of pleasure, of dinner with Davey before he left on the long drive back to Heriot Hills. It was a pity she was going to look such a waif, of course. But even that did not matter a great deal. Davey seemed to prefer waifs to girls with large trousseaus.

She washed her face and combed her hair. She had perforce to put on again the grey jersey dress which was completely sober and unfestive. Then she thought of Nita, and was conscience-stricken that she should have wanted to look festive. Poor Nita who was either tragically a widow, or who had a mysterious husband who was a would-be murderer.

There was a tap on her door and mercurially her spirits rose.

"Come in," she called gaily, "and I promise not to embarrass you by throwing myself into your arms like I did that other time."

The door opened.

"Into whose arms did you throw yourself last time?" Paul asked.

Julia spun round.

"Paul!"

"Why not? Did you think I wouldn't come?"

"N-no. I hadn't thought." It was true that she hadn't thought. Her brain had not been working at all. If it had she would have known that Paul would not allow her to slip away simply like that, to jilt him for a happening that was no fault of his. All her composure, associated with Davey and the deep sleep she had had since morning and the brief but profound feeling of security, vanished and she was thrown into confusion again.

"Do you know about Nita?" she asked.

"Yes. I've been home. I came straight back. I've travelled for hours. It's a dreadful thing."

For the fist time Julia noticed how tired he looked. His face was drawn and his eyes had an unnatural brightness. There was a splash of dried mud across his forehead. He kept clenching and unclenching his fingers.

"We didn't know where to find you," Julia said helplessly. "We thought you would be here."

"I stayed in the flat last night, the one I took for Nita. It's a nice place on the Esplanade. I'd thought she would be happy there—God, what a thing to happen! I didn't know till I got home. I came straight back."

"Yes, you said that. You must be tired."

He took a step towards her.

"Julia, don't talk to me as if I were a stranger."

"I'm not, Paul. It's just that it's all so awful."

"I know it's awful. First that silly woman falling off the balcony and now Nita. But accidents happen. Mother says there'll be a third." He gave a brief humorous grin, a flicker of his old lightheartedness. "Don't let that prospect scare you."

"Paul, this one wasn't an accident. It was Harry."

His frown deepened.

"Please, darling! Not that wicked nonsense again."

"Then why did Nita call 'Harry' the way she did? She screamed it, in that dreadful frightened voice. I heard her."

"It must have been instinctive, as she felt herself falling."

"Then why was the window wide open, as if someone had gone out that way?"

Paul's weary red-rimmed eyes stared at her.

"Was it?" he said, with the certainty leaving his voice.

Julia went towards him.

"Paul, what evidence have you got that Harry is dead?"

"Why, Nita's of course. Her letters and cables from Australia."

"Did you go to his funeral?"

"No, it was too far away."

"Did you see his death certificate?"

"Darling, for heaven's sake——"

"So he could be alive," said Julia slowly. "For some reason he could be in the house. I think your mother knows. Sometimes she looks very frightened. And Georgina. She has seen him. I don't know whether you have seen him or not. I have to take your word for that."

"Julia——" he said violently.

"All right, darling. I believe you. But you ought to find out the truth for your own sake. Because if he is hiding like that he can't be up to any good. You ought to find out from Nita as soon as she is well enough."

"If she is ever well enough," Paul said involuntarily.

"Have you seen her? What does the doctor say now?"

"He says that in the case of such a severe shock there is a chance that memory will never come back. She didn't know me. She just lay there looking at nothing." Suddenly he sat down on the side of the bed and put his face in his hands. "Oh, my God, it's an awful thing!"

And then, just as Julia had been certain that Nita had not been grieving for a dead husband but was upset for other reasons, now she was certain that Paul was distressed not so much for Nita's condition as for the thing that had caused it. Absently she got a towel and wiped the smudge of mud off his forehead, and then, as he clutched her, she held his head briefly against her breast.

"I'm sorry, Paul. It's all such a mess."

"Not you and me."

"Yes. You and me, too."

"But we're in love. This doesn't touch us."

"Oh, Paul don't be so blind. It's all around us, like a spider's web, like those horrid moths that flew in my face with their flapping wings, and their creepy crawling legs. It's spoiled everything. I can't go back. Davey was to tell you. Really, Paul, I can't go back to all that again."

"Do you mean that?"

She tried to free herself from his hands. They were in a vice round her waist.

"Yes, Paul. I do. Let me go, please. It's not your fault. It's just the way things have happened. I hate it as much as you do, going back to what I started from. It's such an anti-climax. But—please let me go!"

His fingers loosened slowly. He had dropped his eyelids so that she couldn't see his brilliant eyes, and he was saying in a flat voice, "If you don't care for me enough to marry me in spite of these unfortunate accidents, which I assure you were accidents, I can say nothing about that. I'm a grown person and I guess I can take it. But what about Timmy? Timmy can't look after himself."

"Timmy!"

"He's been crying all day," Paul said. "No one can stop him. Mother's nearly frantic. He won't let Dove or Lily touch him. And there again, if what you say about my brother should by some utterly fantastic chance be true——"

"Timmy might be in danger?" Julia flashed.

Paul moved his head wearily.

"It just isn't possible. Why should he be? But the poor little devil is in a bad way quite apart from that. You're the only one who could handle him beside his mother."

The cold was coming over Julia again, the slow, inexorable, inevitable cold that gave her a sensation of trembling inwardly all the time.

"If you don't love me I'm not asking you to do anything," Paul was saying in his flat hopeless voice. "But that kid was nearly frantic."

Julia was remembering the time in the night when Timmy's warm little body had comforted her. She didn't want to remember it, but she couldn't help it. Timmy was helpless and sweet and entirely innocent, but he had caught her, too. He was one of the strands in the web. She picked up her coat.

"Then we'd better go," she said.

Paul lifted his head. He couldn't quite hide his eagerness, his triumph. No, that wasn't fair. It wasn't triumph. It was simply delight that she was coming back after all. Poor Paul, she had really given him a bad fright.

Poor sentimental Julia, going back to the nightmare because she couldn't let a baby cry. . . .

"There's not all that hurry," he said. "We'll have something to eat first. Where were you going to have dinner? You looked so pretty when I came in. Your cheeks were pink."

His confidence was returning. (Or perhaps he had never lost it. Perhaps he had just been acting.) He put out his hand to touch her face with his easy familiarity.

"By the way, whose arms were you going to throw yourself into? You never told me."

"I was going to have dinner with Davey before he went back," Julia said, with the calm of defeat.

"Oh, Davey," said Paul indifferently.

"Yes. Would you give him four pounds two shillings and sevenpence. It's the amount I had to borrow from him."

Paul looked amused.

"What did you buy with that?"

But she couldn't tell him about the cheap childish nightdress that a few minutes ago had seemed so sweet.

"Oh, things," she said vaguely.

FIFTEEN

IT was gratifying that Timmy, who had neither eaten nor slept the whole day, should nestle into her arms and take his bottle without a whimper. He had fallen asleep before it was half gone. His woolly white head, tucked in the curve of her arm, was so helpless and trusting that Julia knew bleakly that here she would have to stay until Timmy settled down with Lily or Dove or Kate. Unless she took him away with her. But that would constitute abduction. It was bad enough that she should have to go the long way home, a frightened runaway, without having a stolen child in her company.

Yet did she dislike so much being back here? It was true that she could not bring herself to go into the library where Nita had lain last night, and, although her legs were wilting beneath her, she hated the thought of going upstairs to bed. But for the rest it seemed as if everyone were genuinely pleased to have her back. Even Lily had an almost critical look on her face, and she exerted herself to prepare a hot meal at ten o'clock at night. Though that effort was more probably for Paul's pleasure than Julia's.

Julia ate without appetite. She was remembering how the mocking look had returned to Davey's eyes when he had come back to the hotel to find her preparing to leave with Paul. She had known that for some reason he was despising her, thinking that after all she preferred silk to cotton, Lanvin to Woolworth's. That knowledge had made her too proud to tell him about Timmy breaking his baby heart, and she had let him wave goodbye to her airily, calling, "Give the lamb its supper if Lily has forgotten it."

Anyway, the whole thing was nothing to do with Davey. He had merely happened to be the person on the spot. There had been no reason for him to take anything personal out of any of the episodes. Even out of that kiss meant for a distressed child.

She would never cry again.

Kate, now, was the biggest problem. Lily said she had taken to her bed the moment Julia and Davey had left with Nita, and there she had stayed, alternately crying and drinking cups of coffee laced with brandy. You would have thought Nita was her own daughter and dead at that, Lily had said. When Paul had returned home she had gone into hysterics until they thought they would never revive her. What with her creating, and Timmy yelling his head off, it had been quite a day.

Now, however, Kate was calm, though her face bore the ravages of her emotional upset. Her eyes were swollen and almost closed, and beneath them bags had formed so that it looked as if she had two pairs of eyes, down-dropped and grotesque. She was also just a little tipsy, from her frequent sustaining cups of coffee and brandy. Her words were inclined to slur, and she was much happier in bed.

"Julia," she said in a weak, pathetic voice, "you and Paul will postpone the wedding until Nita is better, won't you?"

"We haven't even talked about that yet," Julia said. This was true, for when she had agreed to come back to Heriot Hills only the thought of Timmy had been in her mind. She had been grateful to Paul for not having raised the question of their marriage again. But it would have to be faced, of course. In Timaru, whether she had loved Paul or not, she had felt she could not come back to the peculiar, frightening, mysterious atmosphere that existed in this house.

Now she was back, and Paul was being thoughtful, quiet and gentle, the way she had always remembered him. If only someone would tell her the truth, the absolute truth of what had been going on, she could be happy here after all.

There were the mountains, of course. All the way back, the larger they had loomed out of the twilight, cloud-wreathed and forbidding, the more the oppression of them had grown on Julia. The wind coming across the low hills was like their chill breath. It was sheer imagination, of course, that they were sinister and that nothing could come from them but storms and death. But there they were going to be, always; frozen, domineering, inescapable shapes. Even on dull days, when they were invisible behind clouds, one would be overwhelmingly conscious of them, like a presence behind a shut door, listening and breathing.

The windows of Kate's bedroom were all shut and the air was warm and fuggy. It might have been a room in a house in a thickly populated town, but all the time, while she looked at Kate's forlorn face and her blonde hair spread untidily on the pillow, Julia could hear the rising wind, and see in her mind the tossed mist over the high crags.

"Poor Nita," said Kate in her slurred voice. "You must wait for her to get well. It's only fair."

"Yes," said Julia evenly. "We must wait until she tells us what happened last night."

"You mean how she came to stumble like that. But probably the poor child doesn't know."

"She would know if someone had pushed her."

Kate groped under her pillow for her handkerchief. Her

little mouth was being drawn down again as if something invisible pulled it.

"But that's impossible, dear. There was no one downstairs. Paul was away and Lily had gone over to Dove's. Nita was quite alone. And she must have gone into the library for a minute because she hadn't even bothered to close the window. I had opened it before I went to bed because those old books make the room smell so musty."

Julia watched Kate's crumpled tear-sodden face. Had she carefully made up that story about the open window? To shield somebody?

"As it happened I was downstairs," she said casually. "I couldn't sleep and I was going to make a cup of tea. I heard Nita call when she fell."

"W-what?"

"She called Harry."

Kate lifted her swollen eyelids, then let them fall again. And her four eyes, the two real ones, and the two little pouches beneath them, were all veiled, so that her face, her crumpled doll's face, looked ridiculously secret.

"But, my dear, that's impossible."

"I have perfectly reliable hearing," Julia commented. Then she lost her composure and sitting on the edge of the bed she grasped Kate's damp soft hand.

"Look, I've got to know. *Is* Harry in this house? Are you hiding him?"

Kate shrank back in infinite distress.

"Oh, Julia! How can you say such things? Harry here, when we've lost him forever. Oh, my dear child, you don't know how cruel you are being."

"I don't mean to be cruel," said Julia patiently, "only I must know what's going on. Paul can't prove that Harry is dead. Can you? Did you go to his funeral? Did you talk to his doctor? Wouldn't it be possible that he left Nita and she was too proud to say so. And that she followed him here. Or perhaps she had arranged to meet him here."

Julia looked hopelessly at Kate's agonized face.

"Don't you know *anything?*"

Kate shook her head. "Such dreadful things to say! Whatever makes you think——" Her voice was lost in sobs. "Oh, porr Harry! Poor Harry!"

It was no use. Resignedly Julia reached for the brandy bottle and poured a little into a glass. Would Kate weep like that for a son who was still alive? Perhaps she would, if he had done some dreadful thing. . . . The brandy quietened her, and she lay back, flushed and exhausted.

"I'm sorry," Julia said. "I've upset you again. Try to get some sleep."

"What—are you going to do?" Kate asked in her blurred voice.

"Go to bed and get some sleep myself."

"I don't mean now, I mean—about this ridiculous fancy you have."

"Wait until Nita remembers," Julia answered calmly. "She will tell us."

Kate buried her head in the pillow, an ostrich in the sand again.

"Make Paul postpone the wedding!" she whispered. "Please!"

The hospital, the next morning, reported that Nita was improving satisfactorily physically, but her mental condition was unchanged. When Paul said he was making the long trip into Timaru to see her Julia announced that she was going with him.

Paul looked up sharply. "I don't think so, darling. There's no need. She won't know you. Besides, there's Timmy."

"I'm going to take Timmy," Julia said calmly. "I think seeing him might bring Nita's memory back. Anyway, it's worth trying."

Paul seemed to have grown older and thinner. The merriment had gone from his eyes and there were hollows beneath them, as if he were very tired. But everyone was tired. Julia herself could think no further ahead than the next hour, and as it went by, the one following. Timmy's bath, his feeding time, breakfast, her morning chat to Georgina who was happily unaware of the events of the past twenty-four hours, her visit to Kate whose head ached too badly for her to get up.

The only thing that had made a sharp impression on her was the fact that there seemed to be relief in Paul's voice when he said that Nita had not yet regained her memory.

Was he glad because she still could make no accusation against his brother? The thought of this strengethened Julia's determination to go and see Nita and to take Timmy.

"I'm sure you won't be allowed to take a baby into the ward," he said.

"Perhaps not, but under the circumstances I think the doctor will permit it. Anyway, I intend to go with you."

"Darling, really, I'd rather you didn't. I'm going to drive like mad, and it's too far for Timmy, anyway. You'll have him in the state he was in yesterday."

"He'll sleep in the car. He'll be perfectly all right." Julia looked at Paul directly. "What's wrong? Don't you want me to see Nita?"

"Darling, don't be absurd. It's just not necessary, making that long trip with a baby, when you're looking absolutely worn out."

"It is necessary, Paul. Anything is worth trying if it will make Nita remember."

"All right. Have it your own way."

He spoke in a sharp clipped voice, and he went away quickly. He was angry with her. It was just possible he was also a little frightened. After all, that was understandable. It was not going to be very pleasant if Nita accused his brother of attempted murder.

But nothing happened. Paul need not have been afraid. Nita lay and looked at Julia with blank eyes. She hadn't any idea who she was. She also ignored Timmy, although he crowed with delight when he recognized his mother. It was only when Paul bent over her saying, "Nita, it's me—Paul," that her eyes filled with tears and she began to sob in a dreary, helpless way.

The sister in charge of the ward, however, said that this was a most encouraging sign, for it was the first emotion Mrs. Blaine had shown. Hitherto she had been completely indifferent to everything. The doctor, too, an earnest young man, was full of encouragement.

"These things take their time. In a few days, perhaps, she'll begin to remember."

"But there's no certainty?" Paul asked.

"No certainty, I'm afraid. No two shock cases are entirely alike. But there's every possibility. There's no reason at all to despair. I suggest your bringing the baby in occasionally. He'll cheer her up, and any time, today, tomorrow, she may suddenly recognize him. It's like a shutter lifting. No one knows just what will cause it to lift or when it will happen. But I do beg you not to despair."

Paul took Julia to the George and asked her to wait there with Timmy while he attended to some business. They lunched first, and although Paul tried to be a good host, even buying a bottle of chianti, he failed lamentably.

It was time, Julia realized, looking from the scarcely touched bottle of wine to Paul's lugubrious face, that they became entirely honest with one another. So far their relationship had gone along in a rosy cloud created by kisses and words of love. But marriage was more than beautiful illusions. She would be flesh and blood and nerves and feelings beneath that fabulous wedding dress. They had to get down to reality.

"Paul, don't worry so much about Nita," she said gently. "She'll get better."

He looked up. His face was unfamiliarly haggard. For the first time the scar from his nose to his upper lip showed distinctly.

"I'm too soft," he blurted out miserably. "I hate to see a girl crying."

Was that how they got round him, the Doves and the Lilys? Julia's heart softened.

"Silly! All girls' tears aren't innocent. They'll put it across you."

Later, however, Paul's spirits had risen. He had been away on his business affairs so long that Julia was beginning to think he had forgotten she and Timmy were waiting for him. But when at last he arrived he seemed to have quite thrown off his melancholy. He couldn't stop talking.

"Sorry I've kept you, sweet. But it's taken a long time arranging about Nita."

"What about her?" Julia asked swiftly.

"Well, somehow I couldn't stomach her lying in that cold, impersonal hospital. I mean, they're all good to her, but in her condition she needs very personal care. At least I thought so. I've arranged for her to go to a convalescent home. It seems an excellent place and the woman in charge

has the highest qualifications. There's a big garden, a beautiful lounge, every comfort."

"It sounds like an advertisement," Julia remarked.

Paul looked at her suspiciously. "Don't you approve?"

"Indeed I approve. If it's as good as you say it will be wonderful for Nita. You were very lucky to find it."

"The doctor put me on to it. It was lucky they had a vacancy. Nita will be shifted tomorrow by ambulance. Oh, and by the way, they think it would be better if she didn't have visitors for a few days. They think now complete rest is the best thing."

"Not even you?" Julia said in surprise.

"I make her cry, don't I?"

"Paul, is that because you remind her of Harry?"

His eyes flickered away, then met hers with a resolute frankness that was slightly disturbing.

"It may be, subconsciously. Some dark channel of her mind. Where's Timmy?"

"He's asleep upstairs."

"Then let's have a drink before we leave." He rang the bell for the waiter and chose a settee in a dimly lit corner.

The lounge of this hotel was becoming a familiar place to Julia. At some future time she would probably have a recurring dream about potted palms, red plush furniture and dark woodwork. The dream would be mixed up with sprigged cotton nightgowns and wedding dresses and anonymous letters and two men, one fair and one dark. Which man would figure in her dream the most? she wondered idly.

The waiter came and Paul ordered double brandies.

"You need it, sweet. You're looking peaked."

"I'm a little tired."

"Of course you are. This has been a ghastly business. But Nita will be all right now." He leaned forward. "Darling, don't let's postpone our wedding."

"But, Paul—your mother has begged us to."

"Oh, she was in a flap yesterday. She'll have got over that by now, I promise you. I know Mother. And tell me why we should postpone the wedding."

"Well——"

"You don't love me any more," he said quickly.

"I—I'm all mixed up."

"Why are you mixed up?"

The waiter came with the drinks. Paul paid him and he went away. Julia leaned against the deep, soft back of the settee.

"I don't know why. Honestly I don't. You're the same. I know that. But it's all those things happening around you, those horrid letters, the moths in my room, and my pearls. My pearls are missing, Paul."

Oddly enough he didn't look surprised. Instead he was regretful and pained.

"I think we may safely assume that the culprit is now out of the house."

"Nita?"

Paul nodded. "I'm afraid so. Poor little devil, she's lost her husband, and she's been madly jealous about us. In fact she's been a little unbalanced, I'm afraid. I've known that all the time, but one had to be as kind as possible. Now the thing has come to a climax, and it's all over. Nita won't misbehave again."

Julia had a sensation of horror mingled with intense relief that at last the thing was becoming plain.

"Paul, do you think she—interfered—with the balcony?"

He looked away. "I don't know. I haven't let myself think so. It's too nasty, that sort of thing." Suddenly he began to laugh unsteadily, irrepressibly. "That poor unlucky walkie-talkie Carmichael!"

Julia caught his impulse to laugh. She had swallowed her drink too quickly, and its warmth and the thought of the indefatigable Miss Carmichael talking unceasingly to Paul all the way to Timaru became immensely funny.

"Paul—we shouldn't be laughing——"

"Hell, why not! We haven't done much of it lately." He put his arms round her closely. His breath was on her cheek, his lips touching hers.

"Paul! This is a public place."

"Who cares? I have to kiss you."

The old trembling weakness overcame her. She sank further into the red plush, powerless to resist him. The warmth of the brandy and the warmth of his lips shut out everything else.

"But, Paul," she gasped in a last protest, "*who* pushed Nita?"

142

"She fell, you goat. She fell."

And since the memory of Nita's terrified scream was dying in Julia's mind it seemed so easily that it could have been a scream as she tripped on a wrinkled hearthrug. Why, she thought, immersed in warmth and comfort, should she torture herself by thinking anything else?

## SIXTEEN

PAUL lifted the sleeping Timmy out of the car when the long drive was over. He looked at him a moment and suddenly said, "I wish it were our baby we were bringing home."

There was both embarrassment and excitement in his voice. Julia, though still a little puzzled by his longing for a child, was very moved. How little she really knew him. His gaiety was only on the surface. Underneath he had deep longings and inhibitions. That was the Paul she had known in England and who had written that beautiful and moving letter. The real Paul, not the one with the roving hands and eyes who was still affected by his long illness.

"It soon will be our baby, won't it?" he insisted.

Julia stepped out of the car beneath the dark trees. The snow-cold wind touched her cheek and her nostrils were full of the damp mossy smell that hung round the house always. She controlled her inevitable shivering, and said with determined happiness, "I hope so, darling." Paul's desire was understandable. After the strain of the war and its associated miseries he wanted something real and tangible. It was wonderful that it should be she whom he wanted it from. That was the beautiful solid thing that existed among all the shocks and uncertainties. Everything would be all right now.

That evening Paul's gaiety continued to grow. Within an amazingly short time he had the lugubrious look off his mother's face. She put on her dark-red velvet dress, brushed her hair into smooth wheat-colored rolls, and put lipstick on her ripe cherry mouth. Her eyes grew bright, and the two ghostly close-lidded eyes beneath them almost completely disappeared. She looked herself, a gay chattering laughter-loving person who no longer had to take refuge in her bed to escape life's more unpleasant realities.

She was extremely affectionate to Julia, and kept calling her "my new daughter" as if she had only just begun to take the intended marriage seriously. Julia had the feeling that if one probed one would still find the frightened person beneath Kate's brave exterior, but there was no time for morbid imagination tonight. Paul's happiness was too infectious. He kept putting his fingers on her lightly, and his eyes blazed with excitement. His fingers were soft and caressing and Julia's flesh tingled. She gave herself up to the prevailing excitement.

Davey was in his cottage writing his mysterious book, or somewhere out in the dark tending newly born lambs. Lily was in the kitchen banging dishes vigorously as she washed up after dinner. Dove was no doubt tossing her beautiful scornful red head at her slow dull husband. Georgina was upstairs in bed, a cozy little cocoon among the blankets, muttering her old tales about her favorite grandson Harry. But she was here happily in the warmly lighted room with Paul; Kate was declaring all at once that there must be wedding guests. It was time they did something about their neighbors. Julia was young and would want a little social life. Besides, there were all those beautiful clothes to be shown off. It would be awfully short notice, but supposing they asked the Longdons from Mount Silver, the Clarkes from Lochside, and the Hunters from the station at the head of the lake.

"A party would be such fun," she said eagerly. "After all those horrid things that have been happening we need some fun."

"Do as you like," said Paul lazily. His fingers, entwined in Julia's, said that his only concern was to make her his bride.

Julia wanted to ask why the idea of social acquaintance with their neighbours had not occurred to Kate earlier. But she knew the answer to that. It had something to do with Nita's unexpected arrival, and the peculiar gloom and tension

Nita's presence had thrown over the house. Almost as if it represented a threat. . . . Now that was removed for as long as Nita failed to recover her memory.

But perhaps the threat had been only intense unbalanced jealousy.

She looked into Paul's sparkling eyes and reluctantly told herself that she understood Nita's feelings. The girl had transferred her love from the dead Harry to his brother. Her fall must have been what none of them had liked to suggest, an attempt at suicide, but at the last moment her courage had failed. Poor unhappy Nita. . . .

That night she slept soundly, and she awoke in the morning with a sense of well-being such as she hadn't previously experienced at Heriot Hills. Timmy, whom she had insisted on keeping in her room, was stirring in his cot and making welcoming sounds to her. Sunlight fell in patches on the floor, and outside the chequered pattern of leaves hung against a background of calm blue sky. It was a fine day, and she was alive and well, Kate had stopped crying, and already in the air there seemed to be the festive excitement of an approaching wedding.

Julia laughed at the cooing Timmy and sprang out of bed. Then she saw the folded slip of paper protruding from beneath her door.

All her light-heartedness left her. She had thought this kind of thing was over. Foolishly she had imagined this particularly cruel pointless form of persecution had stopped with Nita's departure. She had been sure. . . .

But there lay the slip of paper. On leaden feet she went to pick it up.

The black printing said briefly, *Ask where Harry is.*

It seemed a pity to spoil Kate's and Paul's happiness. Julia kept silent during breakfast, while Kate, looking extremely vivacious, her cheeks bright with rouge, her little vivid mouth busy with food and chatter, said that she had spent an hour on the telephone last night and everyone was delighted to come to the wedding.

"They said they had heard rumours and were expecting it," she said happily. "They said it was quite time Heriot Hills came back into its own. They're looking forward to meeting you, Julia, and Paul too, because they don't remember him

145

from childhood. It was a great pity for Granny that your father didn't like the country, Paul. But I can't say I fretted. I'm all for city life myself. Julia darling, the sensation you're going to be in that dress."

"Isn't she," said Paul with satisfaction. He looked at Julia beneath his eyelids and murmured, "Pretty pretty thing!"

Julia could not bear to spoil their happiness. She made no answer.

Kate laughed and said, "Paul, I'm so glad you didn't snatch her in Wellington and deprive me of this fun."

Kate hadn't talked that way a few days ago, Julia reflected. Why the sudden change? *Was* it because of Nita? It must be. As she wondered she was suddenly aware of Lily, gathering up the plates, pausing to let her long, sly eyes rest scornfully on Kate, then on her herself. A slow, scornful glance full of meaning. . . . Julia felt the crumpled note in her pocket, but still kept silent, determined to give Lily, who must be the culprit, no satisfaction.

Paul, now that his ankle was better, had resumed the task of carrying Georgina downstairs. He did so this morning gaily, bouncing her like a baby, saying,

"My, you're getting heavier every day! We'll soon have to put you in a circus. The fat lady of Heriot Hills!"

"So full of jokes," Georgina twittered, her little white head nodding alertly. "How's your wife today?"

"Dearest, you're a little previous. She's not my wife yet."

Georgina nodded perplexedly. The filmy look came into her eyes, like a mist on a window pane.

"Then you should marry her quickly. Naughty boy."

Paul turned to Julia.

"I believe she thinks I should make you an honest woman."

Kate gave her high-pitched laughter.

"Granny dear, they've been thirteen thousand miles apart. Nothing could be more respectable."

Julia fingered the note in her pocket.

"Paul, she's mixed up again. I think she's talking about Nita." Then before anyone could speak she went on, "I'm sorry to be a worrier, or whatever this makes one, but I've had another of these letters."

She handed the slip of paper to Paul who read it at a

glance. Kate, at his shoulder, also read it. Julia waited for them to express their indignation.

For a moment, however, neither spoke. Then Kate's face seemed to collapse. She put her hand to her temples.

"Oh dear! I'm afraid my head—I thought it was better. All this excitement—I'll have to go back to bed."

"Mother!" Paul's voice was sharp, a command. "Don't get upset over a stupid thing like this. I'll very soon get to the bottom of it. Let me have this, Julia." He tapped the paper in his hand. "I'll put an end to this sort of thing once and for all."

Julia was aware of two things, the first that Paul, for all his angry bluster, had had a bad shock. His mouth had tightened into a thin hard line, his eyes were prominent, his colour heightened. The second was that this was the first display of real anger that Paul had made on being shown one of the letters. The previous ones he had been inclined to treat with an indignation that lacked seriousness, as if the offence were childish and forgivable.

He had thought Nita had been the culprit and she could be managed. But now he found he had been wrong, and he was extremely disturbed.

Julia watched his face. "Well," she said lightly, "what am I supposed to ask you about Harry?"

Kate began. "The wicked mischief-making——"

"Be quiet, Mother!" Paul snapped. "Talking about it makes it no better. This time I have to do something. I'm sorry, Julia. I didn't think there would be anything more like this."

"You thought it was Nita, didn't you?"

Paul bit his lips. He muttered something Julia couldn't hear. It sounded like "I still do." But it couldn't have been, for Nita was helpless in the hospital, her alibi unassailable.

Someone had wanted to harm her, she had thought, when all the time it was Nita who was to be harmed. Or was there a dangerous mischief-maker in the house who had designs against them all?

Paul went out of the room and Kate slumped in her chair staring at nothing. Georgina was murmuring fretfully that no one had brought her morning chocolate. Julia looked speculatively at the old lady, pondering on her tiny fleshless hands. Could those fingers grip a pencil firmly? Could she write on a scrap of paper and then silently deliver it to its destination beneath Julia's door? Certainly she had an obsession about Harry, just as the writer of the notes had, but Julia had reluctantly to conclude that the thing was beyond so old and frail a person. Poor little soul, she wanted her hot chocolate. It wasn't fair that a disturbance should deprive her of her comfort.

"I'll get it for you, Granny," she said cheerfully, and went down the long passage towards the kitchen.

But at the kitchen door she had to pause for there came to her ears Lily's high-pitched giggle that suddenly ended in an angry sob.

"I didn't write it. So there. If you're going to believe that then I'd like to give you my notice."

"Ah, now," came Paul's voice, soothingly, "all you have to do is prove your innocence. I'm not accusing you, I'm just trying to get the truth."

"Why don't you accuse Dove?" Lily flashed.

"I'm not accusing anybody," Paul corrected, the impatience coming back into his voice. "Get that out of your silly head. But honestly I can't have this sort of thing going on."

"First it was the salt in her tea, then it was the moths, then it was the balcony," Lily said fiercely. "It mightn't be like you said it would be here, but I'm not one to try murder. I'd like to give you my notice, *Mr.* Blaine."

The accent on the mister was so insolent that Julia expected an immediate reprimand from Paul. In a deceptively soft voice he said, "Ah, Lily, don't get so cross. We understand each other, surely."

"As no doubt you and Mrs. Robinson do, too. Go and ask her to cook for you. I daresay she can do it as capably as she can bandage sprained ankles. And I didn't write that note. So will you stop saying I did."

Julia, on an impulse, went quickly into the kitchen.

"Granny's waiting for her chocolate," she said. "Is the kettle boiling? Paul, what have you been saying to Lily?"

Paul, his face flushed and angry, turned and flung out of the room. Lily burst into tears. She stood at the sink, her hair hanging over her face, her shoulders shaking. At that moment, drooping and disconsolate, she looked exceedingly

148

unattractive. Even her body seemed to have lost its slim grace, and looked gauche and awkward. Poor silly girl, had she come out here, with that drawerful of glamorous clothing, thinking she could seduce the master of the house? She must have been brought up on cheap films and improbable romances.

Julia said briskly, "Come, Lily. There's nothing to be so upset about. It's my fault for making a fuss about that note."

Lily lifted her streaky, wet face.

"*I* didn't write it, Miss Paget. And I don't like being suspected. I've given my notice. I want to leave here and go home.

"No one is going to keep you here if you're not happy," Julia said calmly. "I'm sorry you feel like this. Mr. Blaine didn't mean any harm."

She saw the intensely hurt look that tried hard to be scornful in Lily's eyes, and she said uncomfortably, "Mr. Blaine thinks a lot of you, Lily. But no one expects you to stay against your wish."

Lily sniffed resolutely.

"I do want to go. I don't like the atmosphere in this house. It's secret, if you know what I mean." Her long sly gaze on Julia was full of unspoken thoughts. *I pity you, the bride in this house,* it said, *frozen in that white dress.* "Anyway," she went on, "the country drives me bats. Nothing but tussocks and sheep. Ugh!" She noisily pushed some dishes into the sink. "I suppose he's gone to cross-examine Dove now. Well, I don't know what's going on, but I'll be glad to get out of it."

There was no doubt that if this were to be Lily's attitude, she would have to go. Julia was also convinced of the fact that the girl knew more than she would say. She was in love with Paul, of course. She was deeply hurt, but she still possessed loyalty. She would make her exit with a certain dignity. Paul, with his easy charm, was the innocent culprit. Yet Julia found herself unwillingly believing Lily when she denied writing those notes.

So it must be the red-headed Dove. Which was a pity, because her husband was a nice person and didn't deserve to be hurt.

It was much later in the day that the peculiar telephone call

149

came. Julia hadn't seen Paul since he had walked out of the kitchen after his fruitless questioning of Lily, but he came in at the front door just as she picked up the receiver and spoke.

A voice at the other end of the wire came in a frail sound that scarcely existed.

"Hullo! Who is it speaking?"

"It's Julia here. Julia Paget. Who is that?"

There was a silence during which the wire crackled and hummed. Then the other-worldish voice came again, ". . . the person I wanted. . . . Come and see me. . . ."

The sound faded. Julia said urgently. "I can't hear you. Who is it speaking?" Suddenly her heart gave a great jump. "Is it Nita?"

". . . tomorrow . . . I'll be——" Then there was a distinct click, as if, in the middle of a sentence, the speaker had hung up.

"Who is it? Who are you trying to talk to?" came Paul's voice behind Julia.

She turned, thrusting the receiver at him. "Paul, I think it's Nita. But we've been cut off. She was just saying something and the telephone clicked."

Paul grabbed the receiver from her. "Hullo! Hullo!" His voice was strained, his whole body in an attitude of extreme tenseness. "Hullo!"

Suddenly he put the receiver down.

"There's no one there. Darling, it couldn't have been Nita."

"But why not?" Julia was breathless with excitement. "She could have got her memory back."

"Did it sound like her voice?"

"Actually it didn't sound like anybody's voice. It was so faroff, sort of ghostly. But she wanted to see me, whoever it was."

"Are you sure you heard this voice at all?"

"Of course I did. I didn't imagine it."

"We'll soon see." Paul began to dial swiftly. He put the receiver to his ear, and Julia saw the tension in his face as he waited. He's worried about something, she thought. But before she could pursue the thought Paul spoke.

"Hullo! Is that the Groves Nursing Home? Can I speak to the matron, please?"

A few moments later he was asking how Nita was. Julia heard the concern in his voice.

"No change. . . . But she stood the move all right? Has the doctor seen her? . . . Yes . . . yes. . . . I'm sure you are. . . . Thank you, matron, I'll ring again tomorrow."

He put the receiver down and turned to Julia.

"It certainly wasn't Nita, darling. Her condition is unchanged. She doesn't remember anything, and she hasn't been out of bed yet."

Julia was puzzled. "But, Paul, I'm sure——"

He interrupted her, almost roughly. "For heaven's sake, you can't argue with that. I've just spoken to the matron."

"Then who was I speaking to?"

"A wrong number, I should think. Forget about it."

He slipped his arm round her in a brief embrace. She felt his knee touching hers. She steeled herself against the delicious weakening of her senses. Lily's senses once had weakened, too. So, perhaps, had Dove's. She was no longer sure about Paul.

Twice again during the afternoon the telephone rang. Each time Julia contrived to answer it, but each time there was no one there. Once the receiver at the other end went down with an abrupt and final click and once, faintly, Julia thought she heard a scream, high-pitched and as eerie as the far-off voice had been. Her nerves were jangling. The happy mood in which she had awoken had vanished long ago and she wondered how she could ever bear the house. Georgina, drowsing and snuffling over the fire. Kate giving little hastily suppressed jumps every time anyone came into the room, Lily sulkily turning out the big front room and the hall in preparation for the wedding reception, and muttering about packing her bags to go on the bus the next day, were all part of the unbearable gloom. Timmy was the only one who laughed and gurgled happily, but Timmy was her jailer. He had brought her back, and here, because of him, she had to stay.

"Paul, did you see Dove?" she asked later.

"Dove?"

"About the letter. It must have been she who wrote it if it wasn't Lily."

151

He frowned. "I didn't see Dove. I saw Tom. He says she has been in bed since yesterday with a bad cold."

"Then what?"

"I'm afraid Lily must have been lying. She wants to leave."

"I know. But I don't think she was lying, Paul."

He flung round on her, the colour high in his cheeks, his eyes angry and peculiarly like Kate's in their suggestion of suppressed fear.

"Then who wrote the damned letter if Dove was ill in bed and Lily's speaking the truth? There's no one else it could have been, unless it was Davey."

Davey! To suspect him had never entered Julia's head. Davey with his mocking eyes and double-edged remarks. Somehow Julia found the thought of suspecting him intolerable. She wrapped Timmy in a warm coat and took him up to Dove's with the twofold purpose of giving Timmy an airing and seeing if Dove's illness were genuine.

There was no doubt that Dove was running a temperature. She called to Julia in a hoarse voice to come in, and then motioned her away from the bed.

"I've got flu. Don't bring the baby near."

Julia put Timmy on the floor and came up to the bed.

"Paul said you were ill. I came to see if there was anything I could do."

Dove's green eyes clouded and went sulky.

"What was he doing over here? No, don't tell me, I know. He thinks I've been writing anonymous letters. Well, I don't stoop to cheap tricks like that." She raised herself on her elbow, her loosened hair a brilliant tangled mass against the pillows. "Tom's furious about it. I shouldn't be surprised if he refuses to stay here. But I can't be worried about it just now. I feel too awful."

"Can I make you a cup of tea?" Julia asked sympathetically.

"No, thank you. Tom made me one not long ago." Her eyes went to Timmy who was patiently hoisting his plump little body up by holding on to the knobs of a chest of drawers. "What are you going to do with him when you go away?"

"Go away?" said Julia.

"Surely after the object lessons you have had, you won't

be staying? One way and another I'd say the house has a hoodoo on it. Especially directed against young and pretty women. Look what happened to Nita. You can't tell me it was an accident. The same thing will happen to you. Probably to Lily and me, too. Has it occurred to you that we're all reasonably good-looking? Someone apparently doesn't like the female sex to be good-looking."

"Oh, stop talking like that!" Julia whispered.

"Well, what's your theory? Anyway, nobody can say that you haven't been warned, if you've been having a succession of those letters. I shouldn't be surprised if Nita had no warning. That Miss Carmichael had none, but she was just fortunate. That was meant to be you."

Julia felt the chill coming over her again, so that she was almost physically sick.

"The house has a hoodoo," Dove said in her hoarse voice, then, suddenly, as Lily had done, she began to cry. Her mouth twisted, her eyes grew reddened and swollen. She blew her nose violently, and sank down miserably into the pillows.

"Don't take any notice of me," she gasped. "I'm on a course of sulphanilamide. It always makes me feel like committing suicide."

Julia sat on the edge of the bed.

"Tell me, do you think Paul's brother Harry is here?"

"Oh God! Now you're talking like the old woman. But she's nuts. Or so they say. If Harry is here he must be masquerading under another name and personality. That's all I can think." Her swollen eyes seemed to have in them an intense significance. "Has that occurred to you?"

## SEVENTEEN

DAVEY had just got in from his round of the sheep. His clothes were soaked, his face thin with weariness. Under each arm he carried a new-born lamb.

He seemed surprised to see Julia and said in his soft voice with its amused half-contemptuous undertones, "You've been neglecting us lately. And here I have two more charges for you."

He set the shaky-legged creatures on the floor and watched them stagger across the room. The fireplace had not been cleaned from the previous day. It was choked with dead ash. The room was unswept and comfortless. Julia had a momentary qualm about the neglected state of the place. She had scarcely set eyes on Davey since that afternoon in Timaru when Paul had come unexpectedly, and she had told Davey that she was going back to Heriot Hills. He hadn't believed that it was because of Timmy, and he had despised her for being so easily swayed by Paul's charm, or perhaps by the material comforts that marriage to Paul would bring. He had never been able to forget the extravagant magnitude of her trousseau.

ᐧ But no matter what Davey thought of her, it was too bad that in the middle of the lambing season someone wasn't looking after him a little better.

Then Julia remembered why she had come and she said, "Why do you work so hard?"

"Because I don't care to see animals die for lack of attention."

"Paul doesn't worry very much."

"I'm afraid he's a little taken up with other things at present. It's perfectly understandable."

His dark bright eyes swept over her. Suddenly she was longing unreasonably for the wholly gentle person who had one day dried her tears. Oh Davey, what I suspect can't be true!

"But you wouldn't work this hard if you hadn't some interest in the property," she persisted.

He looked at her questioningly.

"I mean just that. A material interest."

"What are you trying to say?"

She couldn't put her horrible suspicion into words. But Harry could not always remain bodiless and invisible. Some day he had to be unmasked—the man who lived here secretly, who deliberately injured his wife, who ignored his son, who stirred up dangerous trouble.

"Why don't you tell me who you really are?" she demanded. "You say you're a shepherd, but there's a lot more to it than that. Why, even that very first night you made me talk as I would never have dreamed I could to a complete stranger. You were much more interested in me than a shepherd—even if he were a personal friend of Paul's—should have been."

"Naturally I was interested in you. I had a reason to be."

"Why?" she flashed.

"Because you were even more beautiful than your picture."

"Oh, that." She tossed that information aside, then she said quickly, "When did you see my picture?"

"At the time we wrote the letters."

"We!"

"Paul had a poisoned hand. He couldn't hold a pen."

"You mean—you wrote that first letter."

It seemed as if he were no longer laughing at her. But she wasn't sure. His eyes were very bright.

"Does it matter?"

She shook her head slowly. She was remembering that paper she had discovered in his desk with the name Paul written across it, as if someone were practising it to commit a forgery. This, after all, was no forgery. It was a simple act of kindness. Only it meant that that treasured letter was no longer privately hers and Paul's. Indeed, it had never been.

There was no reason for her to feel resentful with Paul for not having told her that. A man was not sensitive about those things. He would not realise that now, in a peculiar way, Davey was mixed up in their life. That the magic of the letter was spoilt.

"You make me think of a seapink," Davey was saying.

"Why?" she said indifferently.

"You're clinging so hard to this cold stormy rocky place. You're even blooming. Those delicate pink cheeks of yours, and that wind-blown hair." He was speaking dreamingly, as if he were writing the words on paper. "Fragile, but tough. Just like that obstinate little flower that out-blooms gales. You don't really love Paul."

"Davey!" Her voice was an astonished whisper.

He put his arms round her suddenly. His hands, thin, hard, and full of vibrant life, bit into her flesh.

"You love me," he said outrageously.

155

She began to struggle away from him.

"Davey, I—Davey, this is fantastic. Let me go!"

One of the lambs tottered against her legs and gave a thin bleat. Davey's eyelids fell. He brushed her lips quickly with his own and released her.

She sat down in the rocking chair. She found that, absurdly, she was trembling.

With complete self-possession he scooped up the two lambs and took them through to the back. When he returned with paper and kindling for lighting the fire he said casually,

"Well, what was it you came down here for?"

She stood up angrily.

"It was to ask you a simple question. I didn't expect this."

He looked at her with wide-open eyes from which every trace of mockery had vanished, and said simply,

"To me you are the most beautiful woman in the world." A moment later, as she remained without words, he added, "Well, what was it you wanted to ask me?"

"Are you—Paul's brother?"

The question seemed lame, and now completely improbable. Perhaps it deserved his sudden hearty laughter. She shouldn't have flinched from his whole-hearted amusement.

"Me the elusive Harry! Oh no, you flatter me! I'm only what I profess to be, a writer turned shepherd. And that's the truth."

"Then why——" she stopped helplessly. His continued amusement suddenly made her furiously, childishly angry. "Everyone knows something except me. Lily, Dove, Georgina, Kate. You, too. I'm the only one kept in the dark."

"You ought to talk to Paul about that." Now his voice had no warmth at all, it was detached and impersonal. "Do you still intend to marry Paul?"

Her eyes, moving from his probing gaze, saw the dusky little Canaletto above the mantelpiece and her baffled anger deepened.

"Yes, I do," she cried. "I certainly do."

No matter how passionately Paul kissed her in the future she would not be able to forget how Davey's kisses were soft caresses, such as one would give a child. A mere brushing of the lips, a mere beginning. . . . How would she feel if

156

Davey were to kiss her passionately? That unsatisfied knowledge, that, too, was going to haunt her.

"Paul," she said that night, "you didn't tell me that it was Davey who wrote me that letter."

"What letter?" he said sharply, his face becoming wary.

"Oh, not the anonymous ones." She should have realised that at present there was only one sort of letter in his mind. "The one you wrote to me in England. You didn't tell me that you had a poisoned hand."

Involuntarily her eyes went to his right hand, and suddenly the thought flashed through her mind that it was a little too much, the sprained ankle, the poisoned hand, the operations to his face.

He frowned a little. She guessed that he was angry with Davey for betraying a confidence.

"It was only Davey's handwriting, darling. And even that we camouflaged. I was so desperately anxious for it to be the real thing."

"The real thing," she repeated stupidly.

He looked at her with his engaging innocence.

"I imagined you would think it important that a love letter had been penned with your lover's hand, darling. Was I wrong?"

"N-no. I did think it was your writing."

"And the words were mine, definitely, so has anything changed?"

His eyes were teasing. She had to shake her head, although uncertainly.

"It has just made Davey a little more interested than he should be."

"Oh ho! Is our dark horse getting ideas? Actually, I can't say I blame him. You're such a pretty thing."

For a moment, foolishly, Julia imagined she could hear Paul saying those identical words to Lily or Dove. Then she remembered Davey's outrageous behaviour, and she moved a little closer to Paul.

"Darling, who *is* Davey?"

"Just a chap I picked up. We liked each other. He wanted to live in the country while he wrote his book—I've told you all that. I took his bona fides for granted. He's well educated,

157

as you can see. He comes from Australia. That's all I can tell you. What's wrong?"

"You said Australia!" Julia exclaimed.

"What about it?"

"Harry—you said Harry——"

His face darkened. He seemed about to speak angrily. Then he controlled himself, and with an effort began to smile in his old light-hearted manner.

"That poor old worn-out subject is now strictly closed. If you think Davey ever met my brother Harry in Australia, I can only say that nothing was less likely."

"I didn't mean that, Paul. I meant——" But her lips were closed by his fingers. And anyway, even before she put the thought into words, it seemed utterly fantastic.

"If Davey is going to put queer ideas in your head he will have to go. Because you're mine." Then he said in a curious, low, longing voice, "God, I wish we were married."

She looked at him in a troubled way. He roused himself.

"Take no notice. But I haven't been able to track down those anonymous letters. Now I'm getting the jitters."

Impulsively she had to kiss him.

"Don't let them upset you."

"But they do. And they throw poor Mother into a blue funk. After all, it is damned unpleasant. By the way, have there been any more mysterious telephone calls?"

She didn't want to worry him by telling him about the two which had produced no answer. She shook her head.

"Thank goodness for that, at least. It must have been a wrong number. I'll ring again in the morning about Nita, poor little devil."

"Lily's leaving," Julia said.

"Yes, so she says. I'm sorry about that. But we'll find another maid."

"I shouldn't be surprised if Dove persuades her husband to go, too. You're losing all your women, darling."

He looked at her with his deliberately merry eyes.

"They're not my women. You're my woman. Remember that."

Kate, however, persuaded Lily to stay an extra two days while she got in touch with the agency in Timaru to see if someone else could be sent out. This, Lily unwillingly agreed to do, although she refused to unpack her bags and also to speak unless absolutely necessary. When Paul appeared she pointedly walked out of the room. After this had happened several times even Kate had to laugh.

"What a devastating effect you have on these girls, Paul. You'll have to keep him in hand, Julia. His father was exactly the same."

"And his brother?" Julia queried lightly.

Kate's lashes dropped.

"Oh yes. Poor Harry. He was the worst of all."

There were no more letters. It seemed it must have been Lily, after all. Paul was certain of it, and so was Kate. As nothing further suspicious happened their spirits rose. Paul laughed a lot in his hearty infectious way, and old Georgina wrinkled her sharp delicate nose and said, "What joke has Harry been playing now? No one tells me. I enjoy a joke as much as anyone."

"Paul's happy because he's being married in three days," Kate explained.

But that only reminded Georgina of her carefully preserved wedding dress, and she had Lily get it out again, and go over the yellowed folds in a search for moth holes. The air reeked of camphor, and old Georgina clasped her hands quietly on her breast as if she were already dead. Although the weather was fine and sunny the chill seemed to deepen in the house. Julia found she couldn't think of the lovely snowy gown in her own wardrobe without imagining being dead in it. She was getting morbid. The nights were too long and dark. She kept listening. It would be a good thing when she was at last married. Then she could lie warmly in Paul's arms and stop her ears.

But nothing happened. Nita's condition, Paul reported, remained unchanged. Even the telephone didn't ring again except for the most legitimate reasons.

There was no one in the house who disliked young and pretty girls, as Dove had suggested. Certainly, if there were, that person could not be Davey, for he had said he loved her beauty. But she had already forgotten Davey's extravagant remarks, and she would not go to his cottage again. She would live through this week until her marriage day.

159

Then, if there were something Paul would not tell her for fear of losing her, he could at last speak.

She was neither happy nor unhappy. Her chief sensation was one of peculiar, unreasonable and overwhelming apprehension.

The afternoon it began to snow again was the afternoon that Lily unpacked her bags and said she had decided to stay after all. Her manner was humble and full of apology.

"I think it would be a bit mean walking out on you just before the wedding," she said to Kate. "I got a bit upset about what Mr. Blaine was suspecting me of, but I guess I've got over that now. I'd like to see you through the wedding if you'll let me."

Humility came so strangely from Lily that Julia watched her closely, and surely enough, when she abandoned her downcast look, and lifted her eyelids to look swiftly at Kate, her eyes were glinting with a queer excitement.

Kate, however, appeared not to notice the excitement, and seized on Lily's welcome offer.

"Why, of course, my dear. We'd be so glad to have you stay. I'd hoped you would get over that silly mistake of Paul's. Julia, isn't that splendid, Lily is going to stay after all."

"How nice," Julia murmured. But all the time she was watching for the flicker of excitement in Lily's slanting eyes, and wondering what caused it. She didn't trust the girl one inch. Some idea had come into her devious head, and now she was planning to unpack her crêpe-de-Chine panties and nightgowns, ready for some plot. Had Paul been talking to her privately and persuaded her to change her mind? It didn't seem so, for Paul exhibited complete surprise when he heard the news, and when he attemped to express his pleasure to Lily she resumed her haughty attitude and marched out of the room.

Julia was angry with herself for her extreme uneasiness. She kept thinking, "Something will happen to stop my wedding," then abruptly stopped thinking at all when she realised that the thought was coming to her hopefully.

It was only because nothing was straightforward. There were undercurrents which everyone strenuously denied, but which existed, nevertheless. A glimpse of the wedding dress hanging innocent and exquisite in the darkened wardrobe made Julia think of a gigantic silvery moth, and she shivered uncontrollably.

The wind continued to rise all afternoon, and the snow thickened, penetrating even beneath the thickly matted branches of the trees and lying on the dark curving drive. By night there was a gale. The wind shrieked eerily, the snowflakes hit the windows with small constant thuds. Paul came in, stamping the snow off his boots.

"We're going to lose a lot of lambs," he said. "Davey and Tom are working like slaves, but we can't get all the ewes into shelter."

He gave Julia one of his possessive, intimate caresses, his hand moving from her waist down over her hips.

"How are you going to like being a farmer's wife, darling?"

"Come and dry yourself and get warm," Julia said concernedly. "I'll get you a drink."

"That's music in my ears. What a lucky fellow I am."

"You'll need your luck," came Kate's voice, almost involuntarily, and at the same moment the telephone rang.

"I'll get it," said Julia. "Take off your wet boots. Paul."

She went light-heartedly to the telephone. Suddenly it had been so nice, with Paul coming in wet and tired and being able to fuss over him a little, with a bright fire burning and lights and comfort to contrast with the fury of the gale outside.

"Hullo," she said gaily into the telephone.

Instantly there was an agitated voice, a woman's. "Is that Mr. Blaine's house? I must speak to Mr. Blaine at once. It's very urgent. Is he there? Tell him——" There was a sudden click and the line went dead.

Paul was at Julia's shoulder.

"Who is it?"

"I don't know. Someone wanting you urgently. We've been cut off."

Paul snatched the receiver, then a moment later put it down.

"It's this storm. Line's broken again, I should imagine. God, what a place to live! Who wanted me? What did he say?"

"It was a woman. She sounded awfully upset."

"What was her voice like? Anyone we know?"

"It wasn't Nita, if that's what you're thinking," Julia answered, looking at his tense face. "It sounded like an older woman. It was a voice I have never heard before."

Paul picked up the receiver and began dialling.

"Dead," he said disgustedly. "The line's down all right." Suddenly he gripped Julia's shoulders. "What did that woman say? Tell me every word."

"She hadn't time to say anything except that she wanted to speak to you urgently. Paul, what is it? Another of your female friends?"

"Don't joke," he said sharply. "It might have been about Nita."

But even if it had been about Nita, why should Paul be so upset? Julia couldn't answer that. All she knew was that the bright happy atmosphere had gone, and that the old tension and fear had returned.

Kate showed it the most because she was always a poor actress, hiding her true feelings with a false effusiveness. She was obviously fighting an overmastering desire to take refuge in her bed. Instead, she chattered continually and almost without sense until, dramatically, the lights went out.

The fire had burnt low, and the room was almost completely dark. Kate gave a quickly suppressed scream, and Paul stood up and felt his way to the door. Somewhere, suddenly, Lily giggled. It was a half-hysterical sound, yet it had pleasurable anticipation in it .What was Lily up to?

Paul snapped off the light switch. A gust of wind struck the house with force, and outside the window came the cracking of a heavy branch.

"That's what it will be," said Paul resignedly. "A tree across the line."

"No, it's not. Someone is playing a trick on us," Kate declared in a high-pitched voice.

"Don't be silly, Mother. You know this happened less than a fortnight ago. We'll have to cut down half of those trees. The electricians warned me about that."

Julia threw a log on the fire, and the flames sprang up,

partially dispersing the darkness. She could see Kate's white moony face, and her hands twisted together.

"We can't be without lights for the wedding," she quavered.

"Why not?" Paul had come to stand beside Julia. His hand touched her cheek. His voice had a deep, excited quality. "A bride by candlelight. I can think of nothing more enchanting."

A sudden, long shudder went over Julia. She was aware of Paul looking at her sharply. Then he must have decided that she was trembling with anticipation, for he sat beside her and continued to move his hand over her shoulders and down her arm. But she was remembering the night of her arrival when he had raised the candle to look at her without recognising her. He had denied it afterwards, but she had known she was a stranger to him in that moment. How could she marry a stranger?

What nonsense—she was just overtired and apprehensive and as jumpy as Kate. She would go to bed. Tomorrow night was her wedding eve. She was not likely to sleep much that night. She must get some rest now.

She would take the fluttering candle to her room and she would not be nervous because Timmy slept there in his cot beside her own bed. His baby innocence was the sweetest and most comforting thing in the house.

Kate insisted on being lighted up the stairs, because the dark worried her. "Ever since I was a child," she chattered, "I imagined those great shadows on the walls would smother me. Look how they move! Oh dear, now I'll be startling you, too. What's that?"

The sound was only Georgina calling in her bird's voice, "Who put the lights out? Was it Harry?"

"It's the storm," answered Kate in a falsely cheerful voice. "The line must be down, Paul says. The telephone's out of order, too. We're quite isolated. They say it happens often in the country. Go to sleep, Granny. Don't worry."

She clutched Julia's arm and whispered, "Do you know, I'm quite thankful the telephone isn't working. Someone has been playing jokes on us, ringing and then not speaking. Twice yesterday it happened. Wrong numbers, I should think. But it could be burglars."

163

"Nonsense!" said Julia. She wanted to say, "Did you hear a scream, very far away, like I did?" But poor Kate was too jittery already. One had to keep everything to oneself. Finally she had learned that.

She went to sleep with the sound of the wind, like great wings, beating in her ears. She dreamt that the wings that had a hard, rough, cottony feel were on her face, at first tickling and then smothering her.

She awoke with a start, crying out. Someone moved swiftly away. It was pitch dark.

A voice whispered huskily, "Don't get a light!"

Then silently the intruder made for the door. As the door opened a faint light, as of someone holding a candle, shone in. Julia thought she heard a faint, frightened giggle. Then she caught a glimpse of the hand resting on the door frame. It was huge and white and unshapely, a grotesque caricature of a hand.

## EIGHTEEN

At last she got a match alight and her trembling fingers held it to the wick of the candle. The small flame showed the door closed and no sign of the intruder. Timmy lay sleeping quietly in his cot. Nothing was changed. The practical joker was abroad again, but nothing had happened beyond the horrible, unspeakable fright she had got.

There was no point in rousing the house, she told herself valiantly. Kate would have hysterics and Paul would try to convince her she had dreamed it. She must endure this, too, alone.

After a long time she persuaded herself to get out of bed and go to lock the door. She felt safer, then, and even imagined she might sleep a little if she could get warm again.

But one never, never got warm in this house. . . .

The candle was fluttering in a mess of its own grease and faint daylight creeping in when Lily rattled at the door and called, "Do you want your tea, miss?"

Timmy awoke and gave his little customary murmur and sigh of delight at the new day. Julia climbed out of bed and once more made the journey to the door. As she opened it Lily's eyes fell on the guttering candle.

"You might set the place on fire, miss," she said disapprovingly.

"I had a fright in the night," Julia said. She remembered that faint giggle she had heard and she looked at Lily's averted eyes. "Did you hear anyone walking about?"

"No, miss. But the wind was that strong. Perhaps it would be old Mrs. Blaine."

"Yes," said Julia thoughtfully. "Once she came in here."

But she knew all the time it hadn't been Georgina. The movements of the intruder had been too swift. And there was that ghastly, monstrous hand.

She began to shiver again. Only pride kept her from bursting into tears.

"I don't know, Lily. I'm frightened of something, and I don't know what it is."

For a moment there was a queer look that could have been sympathy on Lily's face. Then the girl said, "It's still snowing. I don't see how you'll get to the church tomorrow if this keeps on."

Julia smiled wryly. Lily had a peculiar idea of comfort. But the inverted humour had served its purpose and she had herself in control again. She would not cry in front of Lily.

Later, it was Dove Robinson who had that softer gleam in her eyes that looked like pity. So there were the three of them, the blonde, the red-head and the brunette, all pitying her. For even Nita, once, had looked at her with that softened, sympathetic expression. Three women who loved Paul, one of them possessed a dangerous jealousy, yet all of them pitying the girl who was to get Paul. It didn't make sense.

Dove had wrapped herself in Tom's sou'wester and come over to the big house especially to see Julia. In spite of being pale and washed-out after her bout of flu, she was

165

still remarkably attractive, with snow sprinkled on her radiant hair, and her eyes full of that unwanted sympathy.

Julia took her upstairs to her bedroom and shut the door behind them. It was bitterly cold but private. Then she looked at Dove expectantly.

"Should you be out in this weather?"

"Oh, I'm all right now. Just a bit weak. Have you had more of those letters?"

"No," said Julia slowly, "is that what you came to ask me?"

"I thought you might have had one this morning. I think I know who has been writing them."

"Who?" Julia queried sharply.

Dove's eyes narrowed. "Who but the person who's masquerading under another name? I mean Harry Blaine."

"Davey?" said Julia reluctantly.

"Tom saw something this morning," Dove went on, speaking rapidly. "He'd spent the night in the shepherds' hut up Roundtop, and was coming home just before daylight. He saw someone coming down from this house to Davey's cottage. He couldn't be sure who it was. It was dark, and the person was wrapped in an oilskin and hurrying. But what I say is, who would be going down to the cottage except Davey?"

"Wasn't Davey out with Tom?"

"He had been, but he said he was expecting some important letter, and when the bus couldn't get through because of the snow he said he'd ride a horse over to Tekapo and pick up the mail. The bus was stranded there last night."

"If he did that," said Julia, "he wouldn't be back for a long time."

"*If* he did," Dove said significantly. Her sharp green eyes searched Julia's face. "Are you telling me the truth when you say nothing happened last night? Because, to be quite honest, you look as if you hadn't slept at all."

It was on the tip of Julia's tongue to talk about the silent intruder, the ghastly white hand. But how did she know she could trust Dove? Might she not be making all that up about Davey to divert suspicion from herself? Davey! No, it was too horrible!

She shook her head valiantly, and had the doubtful satisfaction of seeing disappointment come into Dove's face. She had made the cold snowy trip down from the cottage for nothing.

"Oh," she said. "Well, I just thought you ought to know I thought you might be able to catch the culprit red-handed."

White-handed! thought Julia, and the grim humour of that almost made her giggle like Lily.

When Dove had gone she felt that she hadn't a friend in the whole world. Why hadn't she trusted Dove? Discussing the thing with someone would have helped. But Dove cast her warm, amorous, green glances on Paul, and that put her on the list of suspects, on the jealous-woman list. Her visit could have been a trick.

Had Davey gone to Tekapo to get some important mail, or was that meant to be an attempt at an alibi? The only way to find out was to go down to his cottage. She had determined never to go there again, but now she must.

First, however, she would write to Uncle Jonathan, telling him everything that had happened. Because now that she was so completely alone, unable to talk even to Paul who gave her devious answers and was never entirely honest with her, there ought to be some record of the truth.

She began the letter slowly, gripping the pen tightly because of the way her fingers trembled with the cold.

I want you to know, Uncle Jonathan, that although you may feel you persuaded me to come out here to marry Paul, I would still have done so without your help. I wanted to come. Paul was the first man I ever loved, and I always hoped to marry the first man with whom I fell in love. Perhaps I am just a silly romantic. I can't tell. For I still don't know whether I shall ever marry Paul or not.

Harry may stop us.

Did you know that Paul had a brother Harry? He died in Australia several months ago of penumonia. He was only twenty-six. They say he died. Yet I am sure he is in this house. I have never seen him. Then how can I be sure he is here? There are various ways, the things

167

Georgina says, the voices I have heard, the way Nita behaved, the notes that are put under my door in the night. If there is ever another note I shall go mad. I can't bear them any more, they are so stupidly demoralising, and there is no longer anyone I can tell about them because I don't know whom I can trust. The funny thing is that I am sure it is Harry who doesn't want me to marry Paul. If the snow hadn't come and shut us in—we may not be able to get to the church tomorrow—something else would have happened. Perhaps something worse.

I am not just being stupid and imaginative. Too many odd things have happened. The worst thing of all is that now I am not sure about Davey. No one seems to know very much about him, not even Paul. Or if Paul does he doesn't tell me anything. At first I talked a lot to Davey because I was lonely and nervous, and he seemed such a sane sensible person, even if he did despise me and call me the Queen of Sheba. He wasn't exactly friendly, but I did trust him.

Now, with the things that have happened, I am so afraid that Davey is——

Julia's hand stopped dead, the nib of her pen stabbing the paper. There was something protruding beneath her door, a folded scrap of paper.

She had heard no sound of a footstep, she hadn't seen the paper slip under the door. It was just there, blandly innocent, as if it had materialised from thin air.

She stared at it stupidly. Then she made a rush to pick it up and tear it open.

The crude black letters were fainter this time, and a little spidery, as if they had been written by someone sitting in an awkward position. They read,

*I don't want to hurt you but if you attempt to marry Paul tomorrow I shall have to. This, the same as the other letters, is meant for your good. If you weren't such a nice kid I wouldn't have tried to spare your feelings.*

Julia methodically put the half-finished letter to Uncle Jonathan away in the top drawer of the bureau, and turned the key in the lock. Then she tied a scarf round her head and put on her loose travelling coat and heavy shoes. It wasn't far to Davey's cottage, but it was still snowing and she could get very wet.

If anyone were watching and thought she was preparing to leave Heriot Hills they were going to be disappointed. Because this last letter that patronisingly treated her like a child was too much to be endured. Instead of frightening her it had made her angry. Tomorrow, in her wedding dress, she would call this bluff.

She had to hurry now, because if it were Davey who had left the letter he would scarcely be back at the cottage. She would catch him in his wet boots and snowy overcoat.

Kate was in the kitchen with Lily. A warm spicy smell of cooking came from that room. Kate saw Julia, dressed in outdoor things, slip past and called to her.

"My dear child, where are you going in this weather?"

"Only down to—only to feed Davey's lambs."

"My dear, do be careful. Don't fall in a snowdrift. It's such a dreadful day. Lily and I are in the throes of cooking. The bus didn't get through, you know. All the food I ordered isn't likely to arrive, so we'll just have to whip something up. Fortunately, Lily is a very good cook."

Julia glanced at Lily whose fair head was bent over a baking dish. She was beating a mixture vigorously, her voice above the beater was only a whisper, "It'll all be wasted."

Kate flung round, her little full-lipped mouth open, the flush high in her cheeks.

"Why do you say that?"

Lily neither answered nor raised her head.

"You mean the snow may prevent the wedding?" Momentarily her voice, extraordinarily, held hope. Then she shook her head and said, "It isn't likely that my son will allow snow to defeat him. He's a very determined person." She smiled at Julia brightly, the fear naked in her eyes. "Isn't he, Julia?"

"Where is Paul?" Julia asked.

"Oh, he's had the crazy idea of going over to the Clarkes to see if their telephone is working. He has an urgent call to make, he says. It's quite five miles.. He'll be worn out. Darling, don't stay down at the cottage. It's far too cold."

"No," Julia murmured, and went out into the snow.

Was it odd, she wondered, that both Paul and Davey had urgent things to do, that took them on long difficult journeys? Did the two facts tie up? But Davey's journey, she suspected, was a blind. He would be in the cottage taking off his wet boots.

The wind had dropped, and the feathery snow drifted down, gentle as a caress. With rising excitement Julia observed the fresh footprints leading down the track through the orchard. She set her own feet in them, noticing that they were an easy distance apart as if someone had walked with short careful steps. They led right to the front door of the cottage. The door was closed.

Julia reached it and rapped sharply on it.

"Davey," she called, "I want to see you."

She waited a few moments. There was no sound or movement from within. From the back she heard one of the lambs bleating. She rapped again impatiently.

"Davey! I must see you."

When there was still no answer she peremptorily turned the handle of the door. To her astonishment she found that the door was locked.

But the fresh footsteps leading in, the scuffed snow on the doorstep! Surely Davey was not childishly refusing to come to the door. She would soon settle that. Determinedly she plunged through the drifted snow to the back door. Under a lean-to the three lambs were tethered and bleating hungrily. The back door was shut. When Julia tried it she found it, too, was locked.

The thing was ridiculous! She knew there was someone inside for the footsteps led in and had not come out again. Thoroughly angry and impatient, Julia began to call and rap at the windows. They were misted and half-snowed over. She could scarcely distinguish any object within. The living room showed her dimly Davey's desk and the rocking chair. There was no fire burning. The room looked frozen and deserted.

Completely puzzled, she groped her way to the next window, that of Davey's bedroom.

She didn't mean to peer in. She was only going to stand there and knock on the glass. It was a movement within that arrested her. A slow movement, a dim white square

170

shape rising slowly against the glass, then another following with the same deliberation.

The hands! The monstrous white hands!

Julia stumbled backwards, staring, filled with inexpressible horror. The hands! What were they doing in Davey's room?

As she stared one of them moved in a grotesque beckoning movement. The cold within her was rising dizzily to her head, making her feel faint. Unable to shift her eyes from the window she took another step backwards blindly, and stumbled into a snowdrift. The cold entirely enveloped her and quenched the day.

## NINETEEN

GRADUALLY objects became clear again, the dark square shape of the bureau with its crocheted mats and long empty cut-glass perfume bottles, the carved bed posts, the rosewood chair with its faded tapestry seat, Timmy's cot, the slightly open door of the wardrobe that hinted at the shadowy space within. Her wedding dress hung in there, like a white crocus just beneath the surface of the cold, black earth. Tomorrow. . . .

Realisation came to Julia and she opened her eyes wide. She was in bed. How did she come to be in bed? She had thought she had fallen in a snowdrift, but here she was tucked up with hot-water bottles and there was a delicious warmth seeping through her weary limbs.

She had imagined it all, the locked doors of Davey's cottage, the lambs bleating, the shadowy movement within and the grotesquely beckoning hands. It was a nightmare. Thank heaven for the blessed relief of that.

Someone moved at her bedside. She turned her head and saw Georgina's tiny, stooped figure, wrapped in fleecy shawls, an angora rabbit peering and snuffling.

"Who pushed you in the snow?" she was demanding

171

with malicious glee. "You should know better than to go out snowballing with Harry. He's too mischievous."

Julia started up, knowing that the nightmare was reality after all.

"No one pushed me," she said. "I fell."

"Ah, that's what Nita said. All you women protect him. I can't think why. It must be his wicked charm."

"Now, Granny!" That was Kate's voice, suddenly authoritative. "You're talking nonsense again and disturbing Julia. She has to rest. She had a nasty accident."

"What happened?" Julia asked. "I fell in a snowdrift. That's all I know."

"And you'd be there still if Lily hadn't followed you down to the cottage. It was very wise of her. She thought something like that might happen. But you'll be none the worse for it, Dove says. I'll get Granny back to bed, and then I'll bring you a sedative that Dove says you should have. She says you show symptoms of shock."

"I must have fainted," Julia said dully.

Kate leaned over the bed. For one moment she lost her determined briskness, and the unmanageable fear showed in her eyes.

"What made you faint, dear?"

Julia closed her eyes, fighting the waves of cold that were sweeping over her again.

"Was it something you saw?" Kate insisted in her low urgent voice.

"Harry's being naughty again," old Georgina declared with her impish satisfaction. "You should speak to him, Kate. You've spoiled that boy abominably. Paul was never like that."

Kate, with an exclamation of impatience, seized the old lady by the arm.

"We know who's being naughty," she said. "I'll be back in a moment, Julia."

But it was Lily who stood over her a few minutes later, a steaming glass of milk in her hand. Her hair, Julia noticed, was draggled and wet, and her slanted eyes had a blazing look of excitement. She was a little out of breath.

"What a job you gave us, miss. You had passed out in that snowdrift. It was the cold that did it. I had to get

172

Dove to help me get you up here. It's a mighty lucky thing I went after you."

"Why did you go after me?" Julia asked.

For the merest second Lily hesitated.

"Because just what I thought might happen did. I thought you'd get yourself into some sort of trouble."

"Did you go into the cottage?"

"No, there's nobody there. Davey went away early this morning to get the mail. He was expecting an important letter——"

"There was someone there," Julia interrupted.

"Someone?" Lily repeated blandly.

"Yes. Or something." She began to shiver violently. She tried to speak again, tried to tell Lily about the ghostly hands, but her teeth chattered too much. The words would not come out. And anyway Lily seemed to be smiling, a superior pitying sort of smile as if this poor little bride-to-be of Paul Blaine's was a pathetic harmless creature after all.

"Drink this, miss," she was saying. "It's got a sedative in it. It's what you need."

She slipped her strong young arm beneath Julia's shoulders and lifted her, at the same time putting the glass of milk against her lips.

"You've got nothing more to worry about. It's all up," she whispered.

Or those were the words she seemed to be whispering when Kate came flouncing in.

"What are you saying, Lily? What are you upsetting Julia about? Give me that glass. I'll see that she drinks the milk."

It seemed for a moment as if Lily were going to refuse. She flicked Kate a glance of utter contempt. Then, with a shrug of her shoulders as if the matter were not worth a thought she relinquished the glass to Kate and went out of the room.

Kate said, "There, there!" as if she were speaking to a child. That made Julia remember Timmy and she glanced agitatedly at his empty cot.

"Where's Timmy?"

"He's downstairs. He's perfectly all right. Dove's looking after him."

Then suddenly Kate was leaning over the bed, her plump sagging little face not six inches from Julia's.

"What did you see, dear? What made you faint?"

"Hands," she said. "White enormous hands. I should know what they were. If I could think, I would know."

But she could not think, beyond realising vaguely that the terror she felt was expressed in Kate's face. Its two façades, the one of gay frivolity and the weeping mask of tears had both gone, and there was only the shrinking, trembling fear.

"Where were—these hands?" Kate asked.

"Against the window. Davey—— But it *couldn't* be Davey!"

"No," said Kate, and suddenly her voice was quite lifeless. "What should enormous white hands have to do with Davey? Drink this, dear. It will make you forget."

She tipped the glass compellingly against Julia's lips. Julia took the warm milk slowly, swallow by swallow. Did it taste a little bitter? Who could possibly care?

"Paul?" she queried at last.

"He's not back yet. He'll come up the moment he returns. You sleep."

The sedative Dove had put in the milk must have been powerful, because almost at once she was asleep, and when she awoke it was dark. Through the window, with its curtains undrawn, she could see that the sky was clear and a yellow moon was shining on the snow. The mountains were etched dazzlingly white against the scarcely darker sky.

It was going to be fine tomorrow, was her first drowsy thought. They would get to the church after all. Happy the bride the sun shone on. . . . Even if the bride were surrounded by snow and wanted to weep because of the dreadful lonely purity of it.

Instinctively she closed her eyes to shut out the angular shining mountains, then opened them sharply at the sound of a footstep.

A flickering light shone on her face. For a moment she could not see who stood beyond it. Then Paul set a candle down and gathered her suddenly and violently into his arms.

A pain went through her head. The room tipped up and down, a pool of light and then a vast dizzy shadow. She was crushed and breathless. She thought Paul's violent angry embrace would finally kill her. She had evaded falling off a broken balcony and dying of exposure in the snow only to be smothered by a too-passionate lover.

*Bride by candlelight* . . . The words ran through her head and now at last it seemed as if her vague apprehension about them was becoming reality. For she caught a glimpse of Paul's hand tightly over her breast and for a dreadful moment it seemed distorted, too large, too pale. . . . A moment, and the flickering light showed her his normal square masculine hand with its gleam of golden hairs.

Then a low ironic voice from the passage said, "Come along, darling. . . ." And at once Paul picked up the candle and went, leaving her in darkness.

She struggled up, bruised and still breathless.

"Paul! Kate! Where's everybody? Somebody come! Oh, somebody come!"

It was Kate who came, a few moments later.

"I'm sorry, dear. I didn't know you were awake. How do you feel now?"

"Better," said Julia. "But as if I'm not quite here."

"That's the way you should feel. Now I'm going to bring you another hot drink and then you'll sleep all night."

"Not another," Julia protested. "They make me feel too peculiar."

"Ah, but you won't be in the morning. You'll be beautifully fresh and rested."

Kate seemed sad and affectionate and almost motherly, Julia reflected, puzzled. She was dressed in a dark-coloured suit as if she were ready for the wedding now. Which was even more peculiar. But since she was being so kind one had to obey her instructions.

"Yes, I'll need to be rested," she said obediently. "I imagined I'd stay awake with the jitters all my wedding eve, but I expect this way is better. Spread my dress over a chair, would you mind?"

Kate hesitated. Then abruptly she opened the wardrobe and took out the dress and spread it over a chair. "There you are," she said roughly. It seemed as if she were crying. Julia wanted to tell her that her own mother had died when she was still a child, and it was so nice to have Kate

175

say goodnight to her on her wedding eve. But before she could do so Kate had left the glass of milk on the table beside the bed and left the room.

Julia looked at the dress dreamily. It was so lovely, so unreal. She would not be flesh and blood, but just a stiff and shining creation of M'sieu Lanvin tomorrow. Davey would not have tolerated her like that, she thought, still dreamily. He would have wanted her gay and alive and shabby. . . . But this was for Paul. . . .

It was only after she had drunk the second glass of hot milk that she began to think again of how, for a moment, Paul's hand had seemed distorted, like that phantasmic hand she had seen through the window. And suddenly, in a panic, she thought, "I don't love him. I never did love him. I can't marry him tomorrow."

She was asleep before she had begun to grow too over-wrought, and it was in a dream later that she heard Paul's voice saying in angry defeat, "I tell you, it was only because she was such a pretty thing."

When she awoke completely at last it was morning, and the sun was shining.

Julia moved her limbs carefully. They felt a little stiff and bruised, but otherwise unhurt. Her head was clear, she felt wide awake and extremely hungry. She began to listen for Lily with her morning tea. The house was very still. She concentrated on thinking of Lily's footsteps and the fragrant cup of tea, because she didn't want those nightmarish things of yesterday to come into her mind.

It was her wedding day and the sun was shining. She climbed out of bed and went on bare feet to the window. Already in the warm clear spring sunshine the snow was melting. The snowgrass was emerging in dry burnt-looking tufts, the matagouri's spidery thorns had broken clear. The trees surrounding the house were bowed with the weight of snow, and no longer obstructed the view across the low hills to the mountains. In the rising sun the high peaks were flushed a delicate, ineffable pink. They were like a blushing bride, Julia thought, and suddenly she was conscious of her bare feet freezing on the floor, and the cold enveloping her body.

How still the house was! Even Timmy—where was Timmy? Julia looked round and saw that the cot which had stood beside her bed had vanished.

She had been too overcome with shock and Dove's sedatives yesterday to think about Timmy. Someone else must have looked after him. But where was he now? Was he crying? Did he want her?

Julia thrust her feet into slippers and put on a warm dressing-gown. She was glad to have Timmy to think of. It meant that she spared no more than a glance for the wedding dress that Kate had spread over a chair last night. She went past it swiftly to the door. If everyone was still sound asleep, including Timmy, she would make the morning tea herself.

Then she would find Paul and he would tell her the reason for what had happened yesterday. He must tell her, because it was useless for him to pretend ignorance any longer.

With this calm resolution Julia turned the door knob and found that the door was locked.

At first she was merely annoyed. She had been much too helpless with drugs and exhaustion last night to require locking in her room. Whatever secret things might have been going on she could have taken no interest in them. She rattled the knob impatiently and called, "Is anyone awake? Come and open my door."

From the rest of the house there was no sound.

The situation was absurd. Here she was, on her wedding day, locked in her room. Nice treatment, indeed. Julia began to grow angry. She knocked loudly on the door. Kate's bedroom was the nearest. She couldn't fail to hear that much noise in the still house. If she slept too soundly Paul, beyond her, must hear. He would be eagerly awake, looking to see if the weather were fine, and if they would be able to drive to the church.

"Do come, somebody!" she called. "Isn't *anyone* awake?" Then, when there was no answer, she began to call "Lily! Can you hear me?"

The continued silence suddenly made her frantic. She beat on the door, shouting, "Why am I locked in? Paul! Paul!"

At last there was a faint sound. Julia stopped calling

177

and listened intently. A faint, shuffling sound came nearer, a chuckling and a wheezing and a panting.

"It's no use making all that noise, Julia. There's no one here but me."

It was Georgina's chirruping voice, coming out in little high notes between the pants and chuckles.

"They've all gone, dear. There's only us left. I'm going to write to Mrs. Bates and get her to come back. Then it will be like old times."

Julia leaned against the door.

"Granny! Please open the door. Someone has locked me in."

The shuffling came nearer. She could hear the old lady just at the other side of the door.

"Oh, my dear, I daren't. Harry did that. He may have been having one of his jokes, but on the other hand he may have locked you in for a purpose. No, I daren't let you out. He would be so cross if he came back."

Julia curbed her impatience and her growing panic.

"Granny, don't be silly! Harry isn't here. If you won't open the door, go and get Paul."

There was a funny little, high, breathless sound from without. Julia realised that it was Georgina laughing.

"Paul! How can I? He's dead."

It was then that Julia's knees grew weak and she felt as if she might fall. What was more, she could hear the old lady beginning to shuffle away leaving her still a prisoner.

"Granny! Please unlock the door!" she beseeched. "Or ask someone to come."

"There's no one here, dear. They've all gone away. Nita, Kate, Lily, Harry. All, all gone. . . ." Her voice was a rising and falling sorrow. Soon she would begin her confused tales of long ago, her pointed face sunk in her shawls, her voice completely divorced from the present.

With rising panic Julia began to wonder if she were indeed telling the truth. The house was so still. It couldn't be that everyone else was still sleeping.

She went to the window and opened it and looked down to the ground beneath. It was a long drop. Miss Carmichael had escaped with only a wrenched shoulder. She might not be so lucky. Anyway, there must be someone in the house. Where would they all have gone?

Even as Julia wondered she saw the fresh car tracks in the snow, winding from the front door to the overhung drive.

If they had been made last night they would have been frozen over by now. They were fresh, the earth churned up beneath the scattered snow. A car had gone away early this morning. Could the fantastic thing Georgina had suggested be true?

But Paul wouldn't go away and leave her. At least not without telling her. Or had he tried to tell her last night when he had embraced her so violently? Suddenly Julia was remembering the woman's voice with its ironic possessiveness, "Come along, darling!"

Had the person who had been writing the letters got him after all? The last letter had said *I don't want to hurt you.* There had been pity in Lily's face yesterday, also in Dove's. Lily had gone away, Georgina said. Had Dove, too? And what about her husband, and Davey? What about the vague white shape in Davey's cottage?

Julia ran back to the door.

"Granny!" she called. "Let me out! I want to get your breakfast. You'll want your hot chocolate. Please come and open the door."

From far-off came the old lady's preoccupied voice. "Mrs. Bates will do that when she comes. Don't worry, dear. You stay there. Harry wouldn't want me to let you out."

Harry! Was it he who had driven them all away? Was she in this great house with only a crazy old woman to protect her from a man who pretended to be dead?

No, she mustn't think that way. She had to keep calm. Presently she would think of a way out of this mess. She would wave a towel from her window and perhaps Dove or Tom Robinson would see it. Or Davey, if he had returned. But she didn't think she wanted to see Davey. He was deep in this thing, or he would not have had that shape with the hands locked in his cottage yesterday.

Davey! He had known too much from the start. He had written her that beautiful sensitive letter. He had waited curiously for her arrival. All the time he must have been laughing at her, or worse.

But why had Paul gone away and left her?

He couldn't have gone far. Presently he would come back and explain the whole thing. She had only to sit down quietly and listen for his footsteps on the stairs. Once before she had waited with nervous anticipation behind a closed door for footsteps. When the door had opened she had tumbled stupidly into Davey Macauley's arms. This time she would not be so impulsive. She would make sure it was Paul who came before she ran to the door.

But the person who came, something was telling her, would be the person who had written all those poison-pen letters, the person who had said *I don't want to hurt you, but if you attempt to marry Paul tomorrow I shall have to. . . .*

Supposing it was the unknown Harry who came. . . .

Paul is dead, old Georgina had said. Julia clenched her fingers The situation was so *silly*. There was nothing to panic about. She just had to wait.

It was mid-morning, and she was at the stage where she was considering trying to break down the door by beating at it with a chair when the sound of a car in the drive took her to the window. She was just in time to see the car disappear on its way round to the front door. She hadn't been able to catch a glimpse of who drove it or of how many people were in it.

A few minutes later there were footsteps through the house, heavy measured ones that went deliberately from room to room.

Julia wanted to call out, but suddenly she found she could not make a sound. She leaned against the end of the bed, listening and trembling. She had dressed long since in the tweed suit in which she had travelled. She had also, in her acute uneasiness, taken all her bags out of the wardrobe and hastily repacked her clothes. Only the wedding dress hung in its frozen purity over the back of the chair where Kate had spread it last night.

Now she was surrounded with bags, and if it were Paul beginning to climb the stairs he was going to look at her

180

in hurt amazement. She couldn't think it was Paul approaching. It was Harry, Harry!

The footsteps hesitated at her door. The handle was tried. Julia strove to say, "Unlock the door—please!" Her voice remained a panic-stricken whisper.

However, as if she had spoken aloud, the lock turned. Suddenly, as if the intruder could exercise no more patience, the door was swung swiftly open, and it was Davey regarding her, Davey in leather greatcoat and thigh boots, his face drawn with exhaustion so that his eyes were more tilted, more mocking than ever.

He took in at a glance Julia dressed for travelling with all the baggage about her. He said crisply, "You won't want all that. Just the bag you bought in Timaru, and that cotton nightgown."

And then the most extraordinary thing happened. All her frozen blood melted and ran warm and glowing through her veins.

"Yes, Davey," she said meekly, unsurprisedly.

TWENTY

AFTERWARDS she remembered that that wonderful blossoming in her body had begun before he had kissed her. The kiss was part of it, but even with no caress at all she would have been full of that heavenly mute happiness.

"Do you love me?" he asked.

"Yes, Davey," she said again.

She put her fingers on his face, and moved them dow the scored lines of fatigue, over his eyelids, his lips. S knew now that this face had always delighted her and t she had made herself deliberately blind and indifferent it.

Who was he? What did it matter?"

"I don't know who you are," she said dreamily.

may have another name. You may have another life. But you still have this face, this body, this personality. What does it matter who you are? You're yourself."

"That could not have been better said." He kissed her again. "You're wonderful. But we'll talk more when I've fed you. You must be starving."

"I am, too. So must Granny be."

"Not Granny. She's in the kitchen delving into cupboards."

"But how did she get down the stairs?" Julia exclaimed.

"Slid down the banisters, I imagine. If you ask me, she's an extremely shrewd old lady."

Sure enough, Georgina came creeping out of the larder, an inquisitive, white mouse caught in a cupboard. Her little pointed face was pink with excitement.

"That Lily!" she said. "The food! The wicked waste! There's enough in there for a wedding breakfast."

"That's exactly what it was for," Julia said mildly.

"A wedding! Guests coming here? Oh, what fun! I must go and dress."

She began to shuffle out of the room, clutching her shawls, nodding her old head in pleasurable anticipation, and Julia had a momentary vision of the old lady receiving the wedding guests, a fantastic figure peculiarly in keeping with this great old dilapidated house.

"Granny, you can't manage the stairs."

Georgina turned, and for a moment her eyes were full of a conspiratorial naughtiness.

"Oh yes, I can, if I take them slowly. But there was no need to tell Harry that. A great big fellow like him could easily carry a small person like me."

Davey had filled the kettle and set a match to the fire that had been left set in the grate.

"That will boil in a few minutes," he said. "Didn't I [tel]l you she was a shrewd old woman?"

["]She said Paul was dead," Julia said in sudden appre[hen]sion.

["S]o he is."

["D]ead!"

[Da]vey took a letter from his pocket.

["Th]is is what I went to Tekapo to get. I rode over yes-

182

terday morning, but on the way back my horse tumbled in a ditch and broke its leg. I walked for eight miles to Doctor Brown's. But then I was done myself, and had to spend the night. The doctor lent me his car this morning. I knew you would be all right until today, but I had to get back before you left for the church."

"Paul dead!" Julia whispered again. She was trying to think intelligently.

"This letter is from the Army department," Davey said. "I couldn't easily trace Harry Blaine because he lived in Australia. So I decided to trace Paul. And this is the answer. Paul Blaine was killed in Italy in the last year of the war. That would be a few months after you met him in England."

Julia sat down slowly.

"Then who would I have been marrying?"

"Harry, of course."

"*Harry!* But he was Nita's husband!"

"Exactly."

It took a little while to realise all that that astonishing fact meant. Davey didn't allow Julia to brood over it. He said briskly:

"Harry Blaine is a very charming and unscrupulous person. We were both taken in by his charm. I can give you no excuse for my gullibility except, perhaps, my subconscious desire for a good story. But you were completely at his mercy."

Julia murmured, "Harry! The ghost of the house! I suspected everyone except Paul. Even you." Sharply she said, "Who are you anyway?"

"Ah, well." Davey's mobile brows rose almost into his hair. "That's simple enough. I was born David Macauley Wicksteed. When I grew up I became a rather successful writer. Lately I've found that success is a distinct embarrassment. So I planned this pleasant anonymity."

"David Wicksteed!" Julia exclaimed. "But he's awfully well known."

"Davey to you, please."

Julia was conscious again of the warmth and the wellbeing filling her. She had to be flippant, or cry with the startling joy of it all.

"If that was a sample of your work I found on your desk one day I can't think how you became famous."

Davey said with some smugness, "You fell in love with the man who wrote it."

"Ah yes. But you've seen what a gullible person I am."

Then they were both laughing and the shock and unacknowledged horror of the moment of discovery of Harry's identity was past.

The kettle had begun to boil, and Davey made tea. When they were drinking it he began quietly and systematically to tell the story.

"I met Harry—or, as I thought, Paul Blaine—by chance. He offered me a job here, and knowing that I was a writer of sorts he then asked me if I would write a love letter for him to a girl in England. We'd been drinking together, and he'd told me just enough to make me feel I was on the track of a good story. He said it had to be a letter this girl couldn't resist because it was most important that she agree to marry him. Well——" his eyes rested on Julia with serious tenderness, "you may not believe this, but something came into me as I wrote that letter. I kept saying to myself, this is the kind of letter I would like to write to the girl I love one day, and then, this *is* the girl I love. That feeling was quite uncanny, and overwhelming."

"I could feel it in the letter," Julia whispered. "It made me come out here." Then she said flatly, "I thought it was Paul's letter."

"Harry was immensely impressed by it," Davey went on. "But when it came to writing it he said he'd hurt his wrist. Could I imitate his hand-writing? So I, gullible still, practised his handwriting (it was Paul's, of course) and finally the letter was sent to you. Then I found myself waiting as impatiently as he for the answer. When it came I told myself the sensible thing for me to do was to get out before you arrived. But things began to puzzle me. My instinct for a plot was uppermost again. Why wasn't Harry making some effort to make the house habitable for his bride, why wasn't he re-stocking the place and showing some interest in it? Why did he and his mother behave as if Heriot Hills were merely a hide-out? Why did he want to marry you in Wellington as if he never intended to bring you here at all? Why was he angry when you insisted on coming here, as if the whole thing were becoming too complicated? He didn't act like a man in love. For one thing, he was too interested in other women, and for another, apart from this urgency about marrying you, he seemed indifferent to you personally."

"He had never seen me," Julia said. "I might have been awfully ill-favoured. He wouldn't have liked that." Suddenly she was remembering that voice that had come into her sleep last night. "It was only because she was such a pretty thing." It was resentful and defeated, but it still held its firm admiration for and susceptibility to beauty in women.

"He was nice—a little," she murmured.

"He was weak and greedy and spoiled and occasionally vicious. But I grant you he had a great deal of charm."

"He nearly killed Nita," said Julia, realising now who the prowler in the house had been, that night in the kitchen when he had thrust her out, the night in the library when Nita had screamed.

"Yes, in a moment of anger because she became difficult. Then he had her shut up in a private home that took mental cases. Did you know that? She was locked in her room. He hoped she would never recover her memory, but if she did he took the precaution of paying the matron of the home handsomely to keep her out of the way indefinitely."

"Oh, Davey, how dreadful!"

"It was dreadful. But Nita was more ingenious than he. Her memory came back and she remembered Timmy. A woman shut away from her baby will become very clever in her attempts to get back to it."

"It was Nita who used the telephone!"

"She tried to. She was always stopped, of course. But finally she escaped. She collected that nice new car Harry had bought her as a bribe and came out here."

The whole thing was becoming clear now, Kate's fear, Paul's uneasiness about the telephone calls.

"It was Nita's hands I saw in the night. They were still bandaged. She had come in to look at Timmy, I expect. But why was she in your cottage?"

"She had hidden there when she knew I was away. Lily helped her. Lily was pretty angry with Harry, too."

"It's all so simple now," Julia said. "I shouldn't have been frightened. But the anonymous letters—had Nita written all of them? What about the one I got while she was shut up in that nursing home?"

"She had become friendly with Lily and had given her things, underclothing or something, and got her to slip the letters under your door. That one had been written before Nita's accident, so Lily put it under your door for good measure."

The final significant fact was coming to Julia.

"Davey, if I had married Paul—Harry—it would have been bigamous."

"It would, indeed."

"Then why was Nita allowing it to happen?"

"That's the essence of the plot. And I'm afraid it's all the fault of your Uncle Jonathan, who meant well, but who obviously is an impractical dreamer and trusts human nature far too much."

"He thought marriages of convenience were neat and practical and satisfactory," Julia said. "He admires the way the French still arrange them. And of course ever since Paul visited us he had set his heart on us marrying, because Paul was Georgina's grandson."

"Exactly. Didn't it occur to you that he might have used a little pressure on Paul, as he thought?"

Julia was startled. "You mean money?"

"In other words, a marriage settlement of which you were to be kept in ignorance in case you felt Paul had been unduly influenced and was not marrying you for yourself alone."

Julia felt curiously humiliated.

"Was it a large amount?"

"Some fifty thousand pounds. It was to be paid into Paul's bank account on the day your uncle received evidence of your marriage."

"But Paul was dead, and Harry got the letter," Julia surmised.

"And Harry was quite unscrupulous. His wife was not quite so much so, but she too was greedy. She agreed for him to go through this form of marriage—providing he could convince you he really was Paul, whom he resembled greatly, the facial surgery which was the result of a motor accident, allowing him a little strangeness—and then they were to skip out of the country deserting you. But with the cash, of course."

Julia felt a ghost of her old perpetual coldness.

"Kate knew?"

"She had to. When you refused to marry Harry in Wellington, neatly and swiftly, so that he could discard you at once, she had to be brought here as a chaperon. She was ambitious for her son, but Kate has only a small, frightened soul. She wanted to call the thing off long ago, especially after Nita's arrival."

"Nita had shadowed me?"

"Nita knew her husband's weakness for pretty girls. If you were pretty she couldn't trust him. And you were. So she tried to scare you off with the letters, and the occasional accident; like the moths, which she must have had a hell of a time collecting."

"But something else happened," Julia said, puzzled. "Paul —I mean Harry—got another letter from Uncle Jonathan that upset him a great deal. He was different after that."

"Ah, yes, he had reason to be. Your uncle suddenly became cautious. Perhaps he feared Paul would be a fortune hunter after all. So he decided the fifty thousand pounds was to go not to Paul, but to your first child. This meant that Paul really had to live with you. By this time he was not going to find it difficult because he wanted you very much. It meant that Nita had to be kept permanently out of the way. You understand?"

Julia shivered.

"Then he really meant to kill her that night?"

"It looks very much like it. He came secretly back from Timaru. He asked Nita to wait for him in the library. Either he meant to kill her or persuade her to go away indefinitely. It looks as if she refused to go away and he lost his temper and made that clumsy attempt to kill her."

"And she," Julia murmured, thinking of Nita's state of undress, "thought he had come to make love to her. What has happened now?"

"Well, that's the inexplicable quality of human nature. Nita loves Harry. For good or bad—and I'm afraid with Harry it will always be bad—she loves him. She is making no charges against him. She's just taken him away."

"They'll never be happy that way."

"I should imagine it will be a pretty little hell. But do they deserve better?" Suddenly Davey put out his arms to her and said, "They're finished. They're done with. They're out of our lives for ever. Let's forget them."

But Julia could not relax yet.

"How do you know all this?"

"Kate left a letter. She had become very fond of you, and thought it only fair that you should know the truth, or as much of it as I thought fit to tell you. She didn't want to hurt you too much. Poor Kate. She had decided long ago that the game wasn't worth the cost."

"And my missing pearls," Julia reflected. "Harry must have taken them back when he realised he wasn't getting Uncle Jonathan's money quite so soon. Nita's car he can still return. I'm afraid the new sheep will never come."

"Does that matter?" Davey looked round the old-fashioned kitchen with its peeling walls and smoke-blackened ceiling. His gaze seemed to take in the rooms beyond, full of dusty furniture, windows rattling, draughts whistling down the stairs. Consciousness of all the dishevelled, dilapidated past grandeur of the place was in his face. "Leave the old place to its memories," he said.

"But Georgina?"

"Dove will look after her until Mrs. Bates comes back. This is her kingdom. I should think she wasn't half so crazy before Kate and Harry bewildered her by moving in. You realise she was too shrewd to be fooled by Harry? That must have been a hurdle for them."

Even as Davey stopped speaking there was a scuttering overhead like mice, or the inquisitive feet of a rabbit. Presently there was a high, plaintive voice from the top of the stairs.

"Julia! Julia dear! Something very terrible has happened."

Julia flew down the passage to the foot of the stairs.

"What is it, Granny?"

"The moths have been at my wedding dress. And after

all the care I have given it. Oh dear, it isn't even respectable now!"

"Wait a minute," said Julia eagerly. She ran up the stairs. "I have your dress in my room, Granny. I should have given it to you when I arrived. It was never mine. Look, come and see."

The old lady shuffled on her tiny unsteady feet to the door of Julia's bedroom. Then her dim eyes rested on the dress blooming like a cherry tree, like a nymph, in the curtained room. Her delicate nostrils began to quiver, the pink crept into her cheeks.

"Mine?" she whispered in her light little voice.

"Of course. Jonathan sent it for you."

"Ah! The naughty man! The *dear*, naughty man!" The eternal coquetry was back in her eyes. She edged forward to reach out her dead-leaf hand to touch the dress. Julia took Davey's arm and led him away.

"That's the right ending," she said with satisfaction. "We nearly muddled it up, but at last it's right. Darling, now I have only a cotton nightdress."

"Even that," he said briefly, "is more than enough."

# The Novels of
# Dorothy Eden

## $1.75 each

| | |
|---|---|
| 07931 | Bride by Candlelight |
| 07977 | Bridge of Fear |
| *08184 | The Brooding Lake |
| *09257 | Cat's Prey |
| *12354 | Crow Hollow |
| *13884 | The Daughters of Ardmore Hall |
| *14184 | The Deadly Travelers |
| *14187 | Death Is A Red Rose |
| *22543 | Face Of An Angel |
| *47404 | The Laughing Ghost |
| *48479 | Listen To Danger |
| *57804 | The Night of the Letter |
| *67854 | The Pretty Ones |
| *76073 | Shadow of a Witch |
| *76972 | Sleep in the Woods |
| *77125 | The Sleeping Bride |
| *86598 | Voice of the Dolls |
| *88533 | Whistle for the Crows |
| $94393 | Yellow Is For Fear and Other Stories |

*Available wherever paperbacks are sold or use this coupon.*

- - - - - - - - - - - - - - - - - - - - - - - -

🐦 ace books, (Dept. MM) Box 576. Times Square Station
New York, N.Y. 10036
Please send me titles checked above.

I enclose $. . . . . . . . . . . . . . . . . Add 35c handling fee per copy.

Name . . . . . . . . . . . . . . . . . . . . . . . . . . . . . . . . . . . . . . . . . . . . . . .

Address . . . . . . . . . . . . . . . . . . . . . . . . . . . . . . . . . . . . . . . . . . . . . .

City. . . . . . . . . . . . . . . . . . . . State. . . . . . . . . . . . . Zip. . . . . . . .

5H